Praise for *The Ice Cream Man and Other Stories*

"There's really nothing like Sam Pink. He's one of my all-time favorite writers, and *The Ice Cream Man and Other Stories* is truly excellent. These stories are abruptly funny; strange in an oddly familiar way; sometimes super sad; always, always generous; and an absolute pleasure to read."

—HALLE BUTLER, author of *The New Me*

"These stories make me feel like I'm eavesdropping, spying. They are the glass against the door and the ear hovering over it, the keyhole and the eye peering through. Sam Pink writes grit and beauty just as they are—no cheap tricks, no overblown metaphors. He gives us true laughter in the face of despair. Give this book to anyone who thinks they hate reading. Give this book to your best friend and your enemies. *The Ice Cream Man* is for all of us, is all of us."

—KRISTEN ISKANDRIAN, author of *Motherest*

Praise for Sam Pink

"Pink's best writing . . . wins him fierce and cultish admiration. Part of this, I think, he owes to his chosen subject. For all the attention political theorists and commentators have lately devoted to a definition of the working class, not much fiction chronicles the sheer weirdness of working-class life and labor today."

—*The New Republic*

"No matter what he's writing, Pink's eye for describing the bizarre daily parade of being a person surrounded by other people and with a brain that won't turn off is by turns hilarious, self-destructive, surreal, precise, and moving without trying to be moving."

—*VICE*

"Pink is a keen observer of the culture of minimum-wage jobs and low-rent studio apartments that is the reality of life for all those who don't find a cog space in today's hyper-capitalist economy."
—*The Guardian*

"There are no easy descriptions when it comes to talking about Pink's work. *Unique* comes to mind, but it fails to convey the ease with which he tackles deep themes like depression and self-loathing. *Humorous* also applies, but it doesn't do justice to the way the author manages to bring readers into his life effortlessly and then shares with them devastating truths, both personal and universal. Likewise, words like *entertaining, honest, wild,* and *self-aware* all do the trick, but fall short because, even if used together, they leave out some crucial element of Pink's prose. The solution to this conundrum is easy: pull out a tired phrase and, as convincingly as possible, say to readers everywhere, 'This is special, and the only way to truly get a sense for what's going on in this book is to read it' . . . More than author, Pink is a one-person movement with a distinctive style."
—*Vol. 1 Brooklyn*

"His stories are unique and true and impossible to put down—what more could anyone want?" —*Los Angeles Review of Books*

"I love the pulse of Sam Pink's sentences, the way they can hold the gorgeous and the grisly and the hilarious all at the same time."
—LAURA VAN DEN BERG, author of
The Third Hotel and *Find Me*

"Sam Pink's writing is exquisitely succulent—it stimulates my intellect, makes me laugh and smile and feel complex emotions, and delights me with its tenderness, novelty, intensity, concision, and surprises." —TAO LIN, author of *Trip* and *Taipei*

"Funniest writer currently working. Funny not in a fuck you for being funny way but in a just being real way."
—BLAKE BUTLER, author of *300,000,000*

The Ice Cream Man and Other Stories

THE ICE CREAM MAN & OTHER STORIES

SAM PINK

SOFT SKULL · NEW YORK

The following stories have been published previously: "The Ice Cream Man" (*Epiphany*); "Blue Victoria" (*Fiction International*); "The Stag" (*Lifted Brow*); "Yop," "The Dishwasher," and "Jumping Rope" (*Muumuu House*); "Keeps You Sharp" (*New York Tyrant Magazine*).

Library of Congress Cataloging-in-Publication Data
Names: Pink, Sam, author. | Pink, Sam. Ice cream man.
Title: The ice cream man and other stories / Sam Pink.
Description: First Soft Skull edition. | New York : Soft Skull Press, 2020.
Identifiers: LCCN 2019036850 | ISBN 9781593765934 (paperback) |
ISBN 9781593765941 (ebook)
Subjects: LCSH: Working class—Fiction. | Blue collar workers—Fiction.
| People with social disabilities—Fiction. | Working poor—Fiction.
Classification: LCC PS3616.I5687 A6 2020 | DDC 813/.6—dc23
LC record available at https://lccn.loc.gov/2019036850

Cover design & Soft Skull art direction by salu.io
Book design by Wah-Ming Chang

Published by Soft Skull Press
1140 Broadway, Suite 704
New York, NY 10001
www.softskull.com

Soft Skull titles are distributed to the trade by Publishers Group West
Phone: 866-400-5351

Printed in the United States of America
1 3 5 7 9 10 8 6 4 2

To Nick, Adam, Jereme, and Tom,

as well as any other stranded crash-lander

Stories 2014–2019

Do your ears hang low?

Do they wobble to and fro?

Can you tie 'em in a knot?

Can you tie 'em in a bow?

Can you throw 'em over your shoulder, like a continental soldier?

Do your ears . . . hang . . . low?

Contents

CHICAGO

Different-Colored Candy

Two cars raced by while I waited at the Milwaukee Avenue bus stop tonight.

One tried to pass the other but couldn't, compensating back and forth too much before swerving into some cars stopped at an intersection.

There was screeching, then a loud smashing sound.

When everything had settled, four or five people got out of one of the racing cars and ran.

I went up to the accident with another guy.

We went up to a car that'd been struck and helped remove two people: a man and a pregnant woman.

The pregnant woman walked a few feet, then fainted hard onto the pavement.

Another bystander came into the street and knelt by the pregnant woman, helping revive and calm her, speaking Spanish.

I stood a few feet away, directing traffic.

Urging some cars forward with one hand, halting some with my other hand.

Everyone did as I directed.

To them I was director and ruler.

Making eye contact and nodding in cases of trepidation.

Yes, you may go.

A car to my left tried to pass but I put my hand up and shook my head.

No.

No, you may not.

When the same car timidly tried to pass again, I did a shrug and made a face like, 'Is this how it's going to be?'

Eventually the ambulance and tow truck arrived.

EMTs loaded the pregnant woman onto a stretcher and put her in the ambulance.

I stood in the street for a second.

Not participating anymore, but still there.

And the traffic moved on its own again.

Glass on the street reflected colors from headlights and stoplights.

The road dark blue beneath.

If I had an 'off' switch, it'd be then that I'd use it.

No, I'd probably have already used it a thousand times.

On the sidewalk, I talked to the person who'd held the pregnant woman's hand in the street.

Basically exchanging the word 'shit' in different ways.

Like we wanted to talk more, to be around each other for a little bit.

But then I said, 'Okay have a nice night,' and decided to just walk home.

As I passed a currency exchange, I saw a paralyzed vet who was always out.

He was in his wheelchair, face covered with dirt and head bent to the side against a headrest thing.

Cubs sweatshirt.

Last time I saw him, he was parked there with a huge pastry of some kind taped to his hand—regular office tape wrapped around his hand and wrist a bunch of times.

'Hi, um, can I have some money to get something to eat?' he said tonight.

His voice was high-pitched, muffled, as though coming out of his sinuses.

'Yeah, what do you want?' I said.

He said, 'Well um, from where.'

'Somewhere around here.'

He motioned with his finger at a place across the street. 'Um, can I have a burrito please.'

'What kind.'

'Um, steak I guess, please.'

'Okay.'

As I waited to cross the street, he said, 'Without the, uh, any hot stuff, please.'

'No hot stuff.'

'No please.'

At the restaurant I ordered, then stood by the register, staring at this bowl full of different-colored candy.

Well, here it is, I thought.

Here is the bowl of different-colored candy.

Yes.

May you all remain who you are through your differences, never becoming your differences.

Yes.

The girl who took my order said, 'You can sit down if you want.'

I sat at a table and stared at the TV without paying attention, to avoid having to make decisions about where to look.

A couple at the table by me laughed at something on the TV.

I turned to look at them, purely reacting to the sound.

Noooooooooooooooooo . . .

Take cover, soldier!

But it was too late.

We'd all made eye contact and it seemed I'd entered into some kind of agreement where we had to interact.

Having looked at one another, we now had to navigate the TV show together—our personal beliefs, our ideas, our selves.

I'm going down, I thought.

I tried to establish a good floor stare.

But it was hard.

My face felt hot, neck tense.

Hold your ground, soldier!

Be brave!

I was about to surrender, get up, and run out the door.

But then my food was ready.

Nice.

Nice determination, soldier!

Hey, thanks!

I brought the food across the street.

The vet in the wheelchair took it with shaky hands.

I squatted with him, my back against a brick wall.

'You want napkins?' I said.

'Um, yes, please. That would be great.'

I gave him napkins.

We ate together on the sidewalk.

Neither of us talked.

I could see him out of the corner of my eye as I stared at the street.

I kept wiping my hand on the inside of the brown paper bag because I didn't have a napkin.

It worked, but it didn't work.

Eventually, I said, 'It's nice out.'

'Oh, just beautiful,' he said.

Yes, beautiful.

Too beautiful for my stupid ass.

After a long silence, he said, 'Hey, there wouldn't by any chance be a fork or spoon in that bag, huh?'

I gave him a fork.

He ate the scraps that'd fallen out of his burrito, scraping the Styrofoam with the fork, arm shaking.

I finished my tacos, wiping my hands on the brown paper bag, then wiping my mouth and face off with my sweaty arm.

'All right, I'm going, man,' I said.

'Okay bye. Thank you. God bless you.'

I took his garbage and my garbage and put it in the bag.

I threw out the garbage in a dumpster around the corner.

I pissed next to the dumpster.

The bubbles forming in the dirt looked like the many eyes of something waiting to take me under.

But not tonight.

No, not yet.

The Dishwasher

The dishwasher fucking hates you.

Whoever and wherever you are, the dishwasher fucking hates you.

It's afternoon at a bar/restaurant in Lincoln Park, and he's standing in front of an industrial-sized sink full of dirty dishes.

There are pieces of every kind of food all over, with a thick underlayer of condiment scum—a colorless foam smelling like the same fucking thing always.

Always, every fucking night.

The dishwasher is frowning, staring at the dishes, holding a sprayer attached to the sink.

It's his job to spray off the dishes before putting them through a machine dishwasher.

When there aren't dishes for a little while, it's his job to stare off, frowning, thinking about how much he hates you.

You and everyone else.

Even theoretical yous.

Anyone, everyone.

You could be performing surgery on his beloved pet and he'd knock on the operating room door and mouth, 'I hate you.'

You could be performing the same surgery on him and he'd wake up from the anesthetic, take off the mask, and say, 'I hate you.'

Because these are your dishes.

Your mess.

A busboy drops off a huge bin of dishes and napkins and silverware and ramekins.

A ramekin is an oversized thimble-looking thing that people use to eat condiments and feel less like idiots.

The dishwasher hadn't even known what a ramekin was for a while.

Someone would refer to one and he'd be like, 'Yeah, definitely,' and just stare at the dishes thinking, *Which one of you is it . . .* while narrowing his eyes.

Someone would ask for more ramekins and he'd bring them a stack of most possible kinds of dishes/things.

Someone would say, 'We always run out of ramekins,' and the dishwasher would shake his head and say, 'Fuck, I know.'

Then he learned what they were and now he hates ramekins for sure.

He knew he probably did before, but now, for sure.

Just like he hates everything else.

Just like he hates you.

Only maybe not as much.

Because ramekins are made one way and can't change.

Wait, he thinks, then laughs, spraying honey mustard out of a ramekin.

The honey mustard splashes out on a wave of hot water and mixes with all the other bullshit on the sink—disappearing but somehow never really disappearing—becoming part of the mess.

The mess, thinks the dishwasher. *We all become part of the mess.*

'Fuck, I'm gonna kill someone, Homer,' he says to the cook.

The cook is on the other side of the room, behind a cooking station and heat lamp.

'Yo, kill they asses, Big Sexy.' The cook snaps his tongs. There is sweat covering his balding head. 'Kill all them muffuckers, Big Sexy.'

'Oh-mare!' yells the dishwasher.

'Que paso, guey?'

'Shut the fuck up.'

The cook laughs.

The dishwasher and the cook had first met when the dishwasher was downstairs wrapping cellophane around a block of provolone and the cook yelled, 'Whatchoo doin bwah!' coming down the stairs, and the dishwasher smiled and said, 'I'm wrappin up that loney, motherfucker,' and the cook laughed, turned around, and walked right back up the stairs, saying, 'I heard it all now.'

The dishwasher sprays out another ramekin.

Then another.

Each and every fucking ramekin.

Still filled at least halfway with whatever bullshit the assholes needed.

Needy assholes.

The ever-needing assholes.

Ever-needing assholes of the mess, thinks the dishwasher—and it seems to him that someone is screaming it in his ear.

Holding the sprayer over the ramekin and spraying the scalding stream.

Right into the ramekin.

Water sprays back on him.

He's covered in a thin layer of sweat and scum.

Feet slowly gliding out beneath him on the greasy floor.

Tired and sore, hands raw from hot water.

And oh, how he fucking hates you.

Plate after plate after fucking plate.

Small plates with shit on them.

Medium plates with shit on them.

Big plates with shit on them.

Shit from the ever-needing assholes.

They say there is an asshole that needs more shit than it gives, the dishwasher thinks in a voice he doesn't recognize, then laughs.

The dishwasher sprays more dishes.

Carving away food with brilliant sprays.

Side to side.

Up and down.

Different techniques and tactics.

Spraying the dishes and then putting them on blue pallets to be slid underneath the doors of the machine dishwasher.

Clamping down the door and hearing the engine activate, the water pour, the shaking of the dishes.

'Homer, the dishes are singing to me, man. They sing.'

'Quit smoking that paste then, nigga,' says the cook, wiping his head off on his shirt and throwing chicken wings into batter. The dishwasher stares at the machine dishwasher.

The machine dishwasher doesn't really do much, just finishes off what the dishwasher starts.

That made the dishwasher think they should sell the machine dishwasher and give him the money.

Because the dishwasher hates everyone.

So much.

The hate slowly pours out of his face all day and night.

A metal ball inside his skull, growing slowly.

Staring at the container of dirty ramekins.

Backed-up ramekins were kept in a small plastic bin off the side, full of water and detergent to prevent congealing.

He reaches into the cold, filthy water.

A clinking mess.

Bullshit all over his fingers.

He places the ramekins facedown on the pallet, then covers them with plates, to keep them from flying all over.

And oh, how he loves the sound of the ramekins hitting against the plates.

Like dull chimes.

It's so beautiful to him.

Sometimes executing perfect rhythms.

Which the dishwasher repeats in his head.

Or adds to with his teeth, hands, and feet.

Or drums to with knives on an overturned mixing bowl.

Okay okay ramekins, he thinks. *Okay you're not that bad. I'm sorry. Okay okay.*

Because it calms him down.

Relaxes the muscles.

One long slow unraveling.

To the dull chimes.

Okay.

And his heart would beat a little faster because he'd probably been holding his breath and finally let go.

Okay.

Okay, better.

He opens the dishwashing machine door and slides out a steaming pallet, slides a pallet of plastic cups in.

The cups.

The cups are different.

He does not hate the cups.

All you do with the cups is dump them out and stack them on a pallet and put them in the machine dishwasher.

In this way, the dishwasher is okay with them.

For they mean no harm.

A server and a sandwich maker come through the door.

The sandwich maker punches in on the computer.

The server screams and makes noises in a baby voice.

'Look how many review cards I got,' she screams, holding them out like a hand of cards.

'Yo, fuck that shit,' yells the cook.

'Fuck that shit,' yells the sandwich maker, checking tickets and opening the sandwich station.

The server bunny-hops over to the dishwasher and holds the cards in his face and yells, 'Loooooook.'

The dishwasher has no reaction and continues to spray the dishes.

The server puts her finger in the ramekin-soaking container and swishes it around a little, making a face at the dishwasher.

'Go get more dishes,' he says.

'YOU'RE A DISH!' she says, and skips away.

And the dishwasher unlatches the machine dishwasher and takes out the pallet and steam comes out and he stacks the cups and brings them over to the kitchen.

'Thanks, Big Sexy!' the cook says. 'Yo why you gotta hide my buffalo sauce though, nigga? Can't find that shit anywhere.'

'I shit in it,' the dishwasher says.

He returns to washing dishes, picking through a bus tub, throwing the cloth napkins into a nearby laundry bin, stacking the plates on the filthy sink and hating everyone in the world, dead/born/not-yet-born/never-to-be-born.

Especially the never-to-be-born.

A different server walks back into the kitchen.

He looks around like a kid lost at the store.

'Oh god oh god, Homer, did you get my aioli or no? I need two sides NOW! This person is gonna *freak!*'

'What aioli, nigga?' says the cook, narrowing his eyes.

'Yeah what aioli,' says the dishwasher, smiling.

'I need some garlic aioli,' says the server. 'I asked for more aioli. You told me you had more aioli. I need it. Where is it? The guy needs more aioli and he's gonna freak if I don't get this aioli for him.'

The cook says, 'Yo, I don't have your aioli, nigga.'

'Who has it then? It's somewhere. Why, probably in this very room exists my aioli. And I need it now.'

The cook yells to the dishwasher, 'Yo Big Sexy, why you taking everybody's aioli, nigga? Haha you gotta stop hiding the aioli.'

'Yo, Homer, fuck your aioli,' the dishwasher says, smiling.

He picks up two knives and drum-rolls them on an overturned mixing bowl, yelling, 'Ohhhhhh-mare!'

The server has both hands on his face. 'Oh god you guysssss.'

He runs back out.

'La verga, guey,' the cook yells. Then he sings, 'She only think I'm sexy when I'm paiiiiiid.'

The dishwasher grabs a plate and sprays it.

Plate after plate.

For hours.

Carving away the mess.

With tireless, heroic precision.

No break.

Feet and legs and back aching.

Mindset of an abused dog and ignorance of a weed.

Plate after plate.

His entire night perfectly described through a list.

A list of dishes.

To be inscribed on his tombstone in very small letters.

Spray hitting his shirt and face.

Smelling like weak deodorant and strong body odor.

'Yo, Oh-mare!' he yells.

'What it do, Big Sexy?'

'Fuck your aioli. I'll kill you.'

The sandwich maker laughs.

The cook—visible only as a pair of eyes below a heat lamp—points some tongs at the dishwasher and says, 'That's from the heart, Big Sexy. I like how you thinkin.'

Then he grabs a ticket off the ticket machine and yells, 'Turkey pesto!' handing the ticket to the sandwich maker.

Another server comes back and sits on the counter.

She opens a plastic container and starts forking through it.

'This fucking guy out there,' she says, eating a grape, 'he orders all these wings, but he wants two of these, one of those, three of this kind. I literally almost lost my mind.'

She has one hand at the side of her head, in clawing formation, eyes closed.

Nobody says anything for a second.

Then the dishwasher says, 'Yeah but it doesn't matter because you're gonna die.'

'I know, right?' she says. 'You guys want some of this fruit salad?'

'Yeah I'll get a littla that,' says the dishwasher.

He wipes his hands off on his pants and walks over and goes to bite the strawberry she's holding.

He makes clacking sounds, biting his teeth down hard.

'Don't eat me,' yells the server.

'Yo, eat that bitch, Big Sexy!" the cook yells, snapping his tongs. 'Eat that bitch!'

The server pumps her hand in the air, wobbling her head and yelling, 'Eat that bitch, what? Eat that bitch, yeah!'

The cook snaps his tongs along to the rhythm.

The dishwasher finds himself staring at the cook.

Oh my little crab, thinks the dishwasher.

He feels something touching his head.

The server is bumping another strawberry against his face, kicking her legs and staring at his mouth.

'You need to fucking shave, you're gross,' she says, making a face of genuine disgust. 'It's like curling into your mouth.'

'Are you eating gum and food at the same time?' the dishwasher says.

He leans over and touches his toes and groans.

The server kicks him on the shoulder. 'Move move! Work!'

And the dishwasher walks back to the spraying station.

He grabs the sprayer and sprays it directly into his eyes until his eyes shred apart and get pushed into his face and his whole face tunnels through his head and his brain slops out the back and slaps against the floor.

Then he puts the sprayer over his heart and grips the lever and it sprays through his chest and his heart shreds apart and goes out the hole in his back and sprays against the wall, the slop slowly slipping down to the floor.

He sprays downward and rockets through the building high into the air before coming down and smashing against the floor directly where he was standing, bleeding out into the drain.

Totally fucking dead.

Then someone brings in more dishes, and the dishwasher stands up and continues working.

He sprays more dishes.

A hundred more.

And hundreds more after that.

Spraying.

Food and filth accumulating around the sink.

Bloated chips.

Shreds of lettuce.

Clumps of pale ground beef.

Chicken wing bones.

Napkins.

A sad Brillo Pad.

Bullshit.

Condiments.

Noodles.

Tomatoes.

Onions.

Liquids.

Solids.

A geography.

Until, eventually, the dishes begin to dwindle.

The dying pulse of the needy asshole.

The sandwich maker clocks out along with a couple of servers.

Only the dishwasher and the cook remain.

Cleaning the kitchen.

The dishwasher has to clean the sink.

Corralling food with the sprayer into a grate in the corner.

He sprays away a few big piles.

Bites that couldn't be eaten.

Orders that didn't please.

'Oh-mare!' yells the dishwasher. 'I'm gonna fucking kill somebody.'

'Don't hurt me, Big Sexy, please,' the cook says, making a praying motion. 'I'm just a simple cook.'

They both laugh.

A bartender comes in, work shirt in hand and hair down, and leans against the counter, texting.

'Hey,' the dishwasher says. 'You wanna run my face through that deli slicer there before you go?'

She looks at the deli slicer and raises her eyebrows. 'Yeah why not?'

The cook laughs and says, 'Hell yeah, kill that motherfucker, girl.'

The bartender grabs an onion nearby and tosses it to herself a few times. 'Let me practice with this first.'

'No, wait,' says the dishwasher.

He grabs a knife off the wall and motions for her to throw the onion.

She laughs and says, 'Oh my god. This is going to be so great.'

She bends her knees and tosses the onion like a softball.

The dishwasher swings the knife with a sound like *shish*.

The two pieces of the onion fall on either side of him.

'Holy shit,' the bartender says, eyes wide and covering her mouth. 'That was even better than I thought.'

'Did he do it?' the cook yells. 'Shiiiiiit. Big *Sexy*!'

The dishwasher puts the knife down.

He lifts up a huge grate and fingerfucks some food out of the drain so the filthy water will go away.

There is always a right way to fingerfuck it.

But you must listen with your fingers, thinks the dishwasher.

'Listen with your fingers,' the dishwasher says to the bartender as she stares on in disgust.

When the water drains, he carefully sprays all the remaining garbage to one side of the sink so he can slop it out into a garbage can.

And then everything is clean.

The sink is shining and ready for the next pointless day of the endless journey.

All that has been used has been prepared to be used again.

The dishwasher stands there, holding the sink with both hands to help his aching back.

His feet burn, hot and blistered and swollen.

And he hates everyone everywhere, even the cook.

No, not Homer, he thinks, looking at the cook's eyes beneath the heat lamp.

'What's good, Big Sexy!' yells the cook, tearing off a length of cellophane.

'How much I love you.'

The cook laughs and says, 'It ain't like that, BWAH. But thanks for playing.'

The dishwasher stacks the last of the steaming dishes on a rack.

He stretches.

His back cracks with wet popping sounds.

He slides across the floor toward the back door and grabs his hoodie off a hook.

'Yo, you leavin me, Big Sexy?'

'Yeah man.'

'Who you gonna kill tonight, Big Sexy?'

The dishwasher stares off for a second. 'I'm gonna kill everyone.'

'Kill everyone, dude!' the cook says in a California-surfer accent, playing his tongs like a guitar.

The dishwasher goes back to the sink and sprays hot water into his cupped hand and washes off his beard, lips, nose, and eyes.

Everything feels better, except now he is more fully aware of that creamy/oniony smell that stains his clothing and skin and hair and beard every night.

The same staining smell.

A disgusting stain at the center of the mess.

Smelling like garbage.

Looking and smelling like garbage to keep shit not looking and smelling like garbage.

For one more fucking day.

Each day, one more fucking day.

'Everyone, Homer. Everyone.'

'Later, Big Sexy.'

And then a busboy comes through the doors and drops a huge bin of dishes on the clean sink.

The dishwasher looks at the dishes.

He looks at the busboy.

Eventually, the busboy says, 'Fuck life, right?'

The dishwasher says, 'Yeah man,' and stares at the bin of dirty dishes like it's a thing staring back at him.

Then he washes the dishes.

Yop

Walking home from work tonight, I crossed through an alley where my friend Keith usually slept, to see if he was still awake.

But instead there were two kids, probably eighteen or so: a girl sitting on a parking brick and a guy in Keith's bed of broken-down boxes.

'Hey,' I said, waving to them both. 'I know Keith.'

'Hey, I'm Samantha,' said the girl. 'Here, du.'

She reached into her backpack and gave me a tallboy.

She laughed like *teh-ha*.

I sat down on an overturned bucket and opened the tallboy.

The other kid said something to himself.

He was drawing on blank postal service stickers, talking to himself.

He talked like someone was pinching his cheeks in on either side.

We sat there drinking.

There were rats running all over—out from dumpsters, under cars—converging and scattering as they fought for scraps.

One much smaller rat kept going in and out of the crowd, moving in small hops.

I laughed.

Samantha laughed too.

'That small one,' I said.

'Yeah, du,' she said. 'Teh-ha.' She adjusted her lips over her braces and took a pull off the tallboy. 'But yeah,' she said. 'I stomped a rat before. It was easy, du. Like, I stomped him and shit, and he went, *Eeeh-ya, Eeeeeh-ya* and then that was it, du. When I checked a few days later or whatever, he was still there just like, laying there dead. Er . . .' She looked up for a second, then nodded. 'Teh-ha, yeah. Then this one guy I know, I showed him the dead rat and he showed me a video of a rat getting lit on fire. And like, it was screaming for a few minutes and shit before it died. I was like, "That's not cool man, nah." I like animals and shit. It was lame, you know?'

I was about to take a pull off the tallboy but I stopped the can by my mouth and said, 'I don't know.'

Couldn't stop watching the small rat.

No one would let him in.

He couldn't get anything.

Come on, let me in, let me at that sweet garbage.

Moving in and out of the group with small hops.

Trying different entry points.

Scurrying.

But no.

The kid who was drawing said, 'Jeeth, that one little guy keepth zumping around and thtuff. Be thweet to thee him zump into a, um, the back pipe on a car, the tailpipe thing, naha.'

I laughed, imagining a small rat jumping into a tailpipe, to the sound of a slide whistle sound, for some reason.

Samantha was looking at me.

She smiled, closing her lips over her braces.

I smiled and looked to the side, took a pull off the tallboy.

This guy came walking down the alley.

He wore tight neon-green pants and a tight T-shirt tied into a ball around the belly, his hair in a small ponytail.

He held out a phone in one hand, gesturing to it with his other hand. 'Please pardon me, but, any y'all need a internet phone? It's a [brand name and model of phone].'

We all said no.

The man breathed out loudly and said, 'Oh well, thanks, have a pleasant eve-nin,' and walked away.

Samantha laughed and lowered her head, shaking her long hair.

I smelled cheap flower shampoo.

She unzipped her backpack and took out what remained of a six-pack of tallboys, broke me off another one.

She took the last for herself and cracked it with the plastic rings still attached.

She laughed like *teh-ha*, then took a big pull and burped, *Yop.*

The kid who was drawing said, 'Jeethuth.'

Samantha kicked an empty forty-ounce bottle.

It clinked off a dumpster and rolled back.

She picked it up.

'Man, du,' she said. 'I've probably drank like, fucking—er maybe, probably a thousand of these. No, like, really, du. Like, three a day every day for the last, what, I've been drinking since I's twelve, and I'm eighteen now, so like, teh-ha, yeah.'

'Fuck yeah,' I said. 'You're the best.'

She leaned forward, laughing. 'Du, I'll fucking slap the shit out of you.'

The other kid said, 'Jeethuth.' Then he said something quietly to himself and smelled his fingers.

Samantha hit the heel of one of her shoes against the ground a few times.

'You wanna hear something?' she said. 'This is insane, er like, I'on't know why I'm going to tell you this. But like, when I was younger—like fifteen, or no, fourteen, or no, yeah, fifteen, teh-ha—me and my boyfriend—he was like twenty-two or twenty-three—we found some baby birds in a nest on the sidewalk. And like, man, this is bad, but we ripped their heads off. Or like no, we cut them off with our skateboards. Because like—I know it's bad, or like, no it's almost good—because once they smell like a human they'll be fucked anyway, so I was just doing it quick for them. Make it painless so they don't have to starve, you know?'

The kid in bed said, 'You could've juth not touched them. Jeeth.'

Samantha leaned forward and laughed. 'I'm a fucking psycho,' she said. She took a pull off her tallboy, hitting the heel of her foot against the ground. 'But nah, I was doing them a favor. And plus like, I was really mad at my mom. My mom likes birds. A lot. So, this is fucked up, but, first I sent a picture of the birds happy and chirping in the nest and shit. Then I sent another picture of them all dead on the sidewalk. Du, it made my mom cry. Her and my uncle thought I's a fucking psycho. My uncle, he like, got so pissed. He made me eat bird meat n'shit. Teh-ha.'

'Bird meat?' I said.

'Yeah, jeeth, like, a parrot?'

'Nah, du, he stuffed my face full of turkey and grabbed me, threw me down n'shit. Sucked, du. But, whatever. I AM a fuckin psycho. Teh-ha.'

Nobody said anything.

I turned and spit, both hands in my hoodie pocket.

Samantha tried to spit farther.

I tried again but all I had was spray and it went back into both of our faces a little.

'Oh shit, du,' she said, wiping her face.

Then she took a huge pull off her tallboy then burped like *yop-yop-yop.*

She unzipped a smaller pocket on her backpack and got out a length of rolled-up toilet paper, then went behind a dumpster.

The other kid capped his marker and put his drawings down and said, 'Fuggit, I'm goana thleep.'

He put his pens and drawings in a backpack and took out a winter hat.

The winter hat was huge; it stood up on his head when he put it on, then flopped over a little.

He grabbed a flashlight from his backpack and got under a tarp.

'Ey, uh, thith make me look paranoid?' he said, holding up the flashlight. 'I thleep with it in caith I have to wake up and bath a crackhead or zumthing.'

'Nah,' I said.

Samantha said, 'Do whatcha gotta do man,'—zipping up her pants and sitting down on the parking stone again.

The other kid lay back in bed, pulling the tarp over him.

Then he sat up quickly, looking off somewhere.

'Oh crap-inthki!' he said. 'I have bologna and cheeth here.' He put his hand on the dumpster next to the bed. 'It'll be good tomorrow right? Ith cooler out tonight. It'll be good. Okay, good.'

He lay back down.

There were crinkling sounds as he arranged himself under the tarp.

All I could see over the mass of him beneath the covers was part of the winter hat and part of the flashlight.

Fuck yeah.

Bash a crackhead.

Eat your bologna and cheese.

Live this fucking moment.

Kill or be killed.

Yop Yop Yop.

Samantha smoked a cigarette.

She told me about how her and her mom lived together but they were getting evicted soon.

I asked when.

'Like, tomorrow, du,' she said. 'Teh-ha.'

'Are the cops coming?' I said.

'Maybe, du.'

But maybe something else.

Something about court and extensions.

She said, 'Fuckin, I'on't know, du. It's like, I mean, shit.' She shrugged, leaning back. 'It is what it is, du, y'know?'

She took a long pull off her beer, continuing half of the shrug.

'I can't stop watching that little rat jump around,' I said, smiling. 'Fuck.'

Samantha laughed, covering her mouth with her hand.

'Man, ahh, my fucking teeth hurt, du,' she said. 'Like, bad. I've had these fucking braces forever man, er, yeah, and my gums are growing over them. Hurts bad, du.'

'Brush your fucking teeth then,' I said, still watching the rats.

She laughed. 'Du, like, I bleed every time I brush my fucking teeth,' she said. 'Er, pretty much every time, yeah. Like, here's what I do every day: I get up, have a smoke, take a shower, brush my teeth, then start drinking. Sucks. Teh-ha. I need a fucking job, du. Hey, this is gross and shit, but like, I just had lice too. I think like, pretty sure I got it from sleeping on the ground or whatever. My mom combed it out though. Wait, hold on.'

She got up and went around the dumpster again.

When she came back, she said, 'Damn, like, that was a hard piss. Even though I came back quick, it was a lot, du.'

She sat down on the parking block again, looked at me.

She turned her head and laughed like *teh-ha*.

I went back to watching the little rat.

The little rat was having some success now, eating garbage left over after all the bigger rats had scattered.

And I must have been doing something with my mouth because Samantha said, 'Are you—do you have that stuff in your lip?

What's it called? Chew?'

'Dip?'

'Yeah, dip.'

'No.'

'I can't do that shit man,' she said. 'Too worried about getting mouth cancer. Fuckin, have part of your jaw removed. I can't have part of my jaw removed, du. That shit's so fucked up.' She motioned with her hand as if pulling off her bottom jaw. 'Fuckin, some monster shit, du. Like, I don't even know, nyarrr, NYARRR. Teh-ha.'

I laughed.

She was trying to cover her laughing with this thing where she closed her lips and nodded.

She lit another cigarette with the one she'd been smoking.

'I'on't know,' she said, 'I'll probably get lung cancer though. Lung cancer's fine.'

'Can I have your backpack when you die?' the other kid said, still tucked in.

Samantha laughed and covered her mouth with her hand. 'Sorry,' she said, trying not to smile. 'I'on't like my crossbite.'

A rat crawled up to where the kid was sleeping, sniffed, then crawled up onto the tarp.

Samantha and I watched.

We looked at each other and smiled.

When the kid noticed the rat, he flung it into the side of a dumpster.

The rat thudded and squeaked, then landed and ran.

'Jeeth,' said the kid, momentarily just staring.

He tucked himself back in.

And everything was good again.

I looked at Samantha and said, 'What sound did the rat make when you stomped it?'

She laughed, blowing out a drag from her cigarette a little more quickly.

She rubbed the cherry of her cigarette off on the ground.

She put the cigarette behind her ear, took a pull of her tallboy and went, 'Eeeeeh-ya, eeeeeeeeh ya.'

Blue Victoria

This was years ago.

In Bucktown, Chicago.

Early spring.

A little snow left in the grass outside our building, but otherwise warmer and rainy.

The smell of dirt.

Gray puddles.

Chris and Victoria and I stood around in the kitchen.

They were leaning against the kitchen sink, holding each other, smoking and drinking.

I was rolling a joint at the kitchen table.

The kitchen, as well as the rest of the apartment, was filthy and full of shit.

And not in a cool/fun way.

In a very embarrassing way.

Garbage bags, dirty dishes, mail, bottles, bullshit.

'The place looks great you guys,' Victoria said, smiling.

She looked down.

She was always hiding her missing front tooth.

She wore a giant sweatshirt that said CANCUN on it with sail-boats, hair in a greasy side ponytail.

She was a baker.

Lived alone a couple blocks away but was always over.

'Yeah I've been meaning to clean,' I said, licking the rolling paper.

Chris laughed. 'Buh HA.'

He laughed like a hyena.

Tight jeans, gold high-top shoes, and a haircut like an anime character.

I'd known him since I was fifteen.

Met him through our other roommate, Robby, who I'd known since I was twelve.

Robby was my only childhood friend and, aside from Chris, the only person I kept in touch with.

But you don't really keep in touch with Chris.

Hyenas keep in touch with you.

'B'HA,' he laughed, gesturing to Robby's door. 'Has the landlord seen that yet?'

Robby's door had cereal box covers taped all over it, hiding huge holes.

One night, shortly after we'd moved in, Robby had a girl over.

And she got mad at him for drinking too much so she locked him out of his room.

He punched through the door and calmly opened it, grabbed his pillow and slept on the couch.

After that, we just kept punching and kicking holes in the door.

The cereal boxes gave it the semblance of form in case the landlady came by.

'We're fucking useless,' Chris said, laughing again.

He tossed his bottle onto an overflowing trash can, where it balanced for a second, then rolled off and hit the ground, unbroken.

We watched the bottle complete its roll.

I finished the joint and grabbed a football off the table.

The football was one of our only non-clothing/furniture/garbage–related possessions.

So yes, we took good care of it.

It was our roommate.

Our sibling.

I threw the football at Robby's door, where it clacked hollowly and bounced around on the floor a couple times.

The door swung back, blocking the entrance to the living room.

'That fuckin door,' I said, shaking my head. 'Had it up to here with that door.'

Victoria was smiling with her lips closed.

I grabbed the football and lined up to hike in the middle of the kitchen.

Chris lined up a few feet behind me and yelled, 'Hike!'

I hiked and ran straight toward the door.

He passed.

No spiral at all.

Flying sideways but on mark.

A 'dead duck.'

I jumped backward and caught the football as I went through the door, tearing it off the hinges except for one small piece.

Chris and Victoria laughed.

I got up and returned to the kitchen, touching my back and checking my fingers for blood.

Chris hugged Victoria from the side and kissed her cheek.

She moved away a little, smiling.

I lit the joint.

Robby had left us a small rock too, which Chris pinched out of its bag into an overturned Frisbee.

'Where's stupid, anyway?' he said, mashing the rock with his license.

It was unsettling to watch.

Like a fly.

Like something else.

I tried not to watch but I kept watching.

I took out my flip phone and said, 'He told me he was getting groceries on his way home.'

And we took turns sniffing little piles.

I decided immediately that I shouldn't do coke anymore.

Chris complained about his aquarium-cleaning job, leaning against the counter and ashing into an empty bottle.

He was still wearing his work shirt, which featured a fish with three bubbles coming out of its mouth and the name/number of an aquarium-cleaning place in Old Town.

He was always complaining.

Victoria and I took turns making fun of his every complaint.

To which he'd respond, 'I know,' while nodding and looking at the floor, laughing like a hyena.

Smoking.

Moving his lips around and gnashing his teeth.

'The shirt is stupid as well,' said Victoria quietly.

Everyone laughed.

'I know,' Chris said.

Robby came up the back stairs, holding a bunch of bags, cigarette in his mouth.

Everyone said hi.

'Hi there,' he said, smiling.

'Yo Robby,' said Chris. 'We fixed your door.'

Robby lifted his sunglasses and saw the broken door.

He clapped his hands once.

'Neheh, awesome,' he said. 'Nice work.'

I handed him the part of the joint we'd saved.

He talked about all the research he'd done at work that day, not for his clients, but about marinading.

He'd just started working as a lawyer and had some money.

And he'd taken an interest in grilling.

Which he began doing for us, almost nightly.

Robby sniffed some coke out of the Frisbee and explained how his views on marinading had advanced.

Oh, how they'd advanced.

We all walked down the back stairs, carrying supplies.

The night ahead of us and no real fate.

*

The lot next door was empty and abandoned—overgrown and partially hidden from the street by a broken fence and some tree limbs.

So we took it over.

Robby set up a couple grills and a smoker and some cheap-ass lawn chairs.

There were a ton of rats at first but then they all moved to the alley.

We'd hang out, grilling, throwing the football, or just sitting in lawn chairs getting high.

Sometimes Victoria and I scavenged for treasure.

There'd been a building there before.

Which meant so much treasure.

Mostly old beer bottles.

But all kinds of other shit too.

We found bricks.

Tile.

A handle for a faucet.

All kinds of shit.

Like the lot was a stage in the middle of endless darkness, from which treasures emerged.

Handed to us by adoring gods.

To do with as we pleased.

And yes, we were pleased.

Our favorite thing to do, though, was skeet shooting.

One of us would toss an empty bottle high up into the air and the other person tried to hit it with the football.

Victoria and I played a lot.

She liked throwing the bottles up.

I liked throwing the football.

'Ready?' she said.

It was Memorial Day.

Robby was grilling, Sox game on the radio.

Chris at the liquor store.

'Go ahead,' I said.

Victoria threw the bottle high into the air from behind.

I got a good eye on it, then threw.

The football connected, driving the bottle into our building.

Kish.

Victoria and I laughed.

'Nice,' she said.

Robby turned and held up a pointer finger while covering the mouthpiece of his phone with the other hand.

'Do you wanna do another one or look for more treasure?' said Victoria.

And we went into the weeds to look for more treasure.

There always seemed to be more.

I thought it would never run out.

'Think I got something,' I said.

Victoria came high-stepping over, swishing weeds and breaking sticks.

She wore a giant sweatshirt with a cartoon character on it and stretch pants, hair in a side ponytail.

She waved some bugs away from her face.

I lifted a piece of plywood with my boot and showed her a couple rusted cans of spray paint.

A huge spider ran away, going into the weeds.

'Well,' Victoria said, her eyes smiling. 'Are we gonna smash'em or what?'

We flipped the piece of plywood up against the fence with our feet.

I grabbed a can of spray paint and set it sideways on a tree stump.

We'd found a giant stone recently too, an orb of concrete that must've been a staircase decoration or light post topper.

Size of a basketball and weighing probably thirty pounds.

The bashing stone.

I grabbed the bashing stone and handed it to Victoria.

She struggled, lifting the stone.

'Juhhhhhhhhhhhrop the stuhhhhyoan,' I yelled.

Robby raised the tongs and, without turning, replied, 'Juhhh-hhrop, nnnnntha, styoannnnnnnn.'

Victoria dropped the bashing stone on the spray paint bottle, which exploded rust-colored grease, *voonk.*

We laughed.

We busted the rest of the cans then split one of her cigarettes.

'Oh I brought this for you,' she said.

She lifted her sweatshirt, uncovering a fanny pack.

She unzipped the fanny pack and took out a book.

It was a book of poems she wanted me to read.

Rainer Maria Rilke.

We'd been talking about books a lot.

She was trying to go back to school and I was writing a book.

'Cool, thank you,' I said, looking at it. 'First pie, and now this.'

She'd brought us pie from her bakery too.

'Yeah, I figured you'd like it,' she said, still looking at the book.

Victoria.

She laughed and looked down.

And for a moment I was convinced her front tooth was lost somewhere in the lot.

And that we could find it and put it back in her mouth if she wanted.

In the empty lot.

Scent of smoke in the air.

Sox game on the radio.

And no real fate.

Chris came through the alley and into the lot, pinning a case of beer to his hip, smoking a cigarette.

He was in a bad mood about losing some bet.

He was already an idiot about money and now he'd lost what little he had for the week.

He asked Victoria if she'd bought him cigarettes like he'd asked.

'Oh,' she said. 'No, I forgot.'

He shook his head and rubbed his neck. 'What the fuck. I would've just gotten them now while I was out. Goddamnit. You said you were gonna get them. God*damn*it, juhhhh.'

He went inside to put the beer in the fridge.

Victoria followed.

Robby opened the foil around a piece of fish and said, 'What a cock.'

'Yeah I hate that guy,' I said, smiling.

Robby laughed like *neh heh* and hit the grill with his tongs.

I surveyed the grill while he explained everything he was doing, as well as what he would be doing differently next time.

'Thanks for dinner,' I said.

We could hear Chris and Victoria arguing inside, muffled but getting louder.

Then they were yelling.

Robby and I did coke out of the Frisbee.

I decided I shouldn't do coke anymore because I didn't really enjoy it.

I decided that was true about so many other things.

But not everything.

Victoria and Chris came outside and sat quietly in their lawn chairs, drinking.

Victoria stared ahead at the ground somewhere while Chris looked at his phone.

It was about to get dark.

*

I couldn't sleep that night, was grinding my teeth and completely awake.

Plus, my room was technically a closet beneath the stairway to the entire building.

We lived on the first floor and the front steps led up over my ceiling.

So I heard booming footsteps at random throughout the night.

TOK TOK TOK TOK TOK TOK.

KAJUNG, the front door slamming.

TOK TOK TOK TOK TOK.

I lay there looking up.

Listening to the ongoing world, dancing on my coffin lid.

I didn't have electricity in my room but there was a tiny window.

I tried reading the Rilke book by streetlight.

But I couldn't focus.

So at the first dim sign of light, I got up.

I put on sweatpants, a hoodie, and my boots, and walked through the trashed kitchen.

Everyone was still asleep.

I went outside to the lot.

Cigarette butts.

Paper plates.

Lengths of paper towel.

Empty charcoal bags.

Flattened spray paint bottles.

It felt comfortable and secure and vital.

Like something I'd defend.

I located the bashing stone and started doing exercises with it.

Lifted it over my head a couple times with each hand.

Picked it up and held it chest level while squatting.

I lay with my back on a tree stump and bench-pressed it.

My blood began moving and I felt better.

In the cool, spring morning air.

Someone came stomping down the back stairs.

Victoria.

She tightened her side ponytail, cigarette in mouth.

She visored her eyes and waved.

'What are you doing?' she said.

'What are *you* doing?' I said.

'Going to work,' she said, closing the back gate. 'Do you like donuts?'

'Yeah.'

I picked up the bashing stone and threw it into the air as high as I could.

It thudded dully in the wet dirt.

Fump.

Resting in place.

No real fate.

*

Victoria and I were on coke in the kitchen, talking about the last book she'd lent me and eating from a five-pound bag of candy.

It was close to Halloween but still warm out.

Robby came in and out of the kitchen, moving shit around, executing a recently researched mustard sauce.

'Ha, you guys still fuckin with that bag of candy?' he said, cigarette in mouth, tearing off a length of tinfoil.

He wore an oven mitt and apron.

His apron featured a pig winking, the phrase 'I smoke u butt' handwritten in marker beneath it.

Backward Bears hat and aviators.

He told us he'd lost part of a tooth the first night he got the bag of candy. 'Like halfway through the bag. I didn't wanna go to the dentist so I just filed down the sharp part neh heh heh. Like new.'

Robby.

He did some coke, explaining how he learned about mustard sauces from this barbecuing show on public access TV, one of the only channels we got.

The show was called *BBQU.*

I'd wake up on the weekends to him, hungover, smoking ciga-rettes and watching *BBQU.*

'Time to find out if my research . . . cuts the mustard,' Robby said.

He went outside.

Victoria laughed like *tssss,* looking down.

She was wearing a sweatshirt with a stretched-out collar that showed her shoulder.

On her right shoulder there was a tattoo of a peacock.

'I like that tattoo,' I said.

She asked me if I'd read Flannery O'Connor.

She said Flannery O'Connor was her favorite, and that I should read her.

I asked her what book to read first and she debated it aloud to herself, looking at either the floor or the ceiling.

She was so high.

'Are you high?' I said.

She laughed and looked down.

I got a text message from Robby that said, 'Hey can you bring the rest of that shit on the counter.'

Victoria and I carried stuff outside—tinfoil, spices, the giant bag of candy, and the football.

Geared up.

Victoria threw bottles up for me to hit with the football while Robby cooked, on the phone with a girl he'd just started seeing.

Bears game on the radio.

Getting much cooler at night, but still nice out.

Victoria threw a bottle up and I hit it with the football and it fell into the grass somewhere.

She ran to get it, doing a few skips.

I went inside to take a piss.

Chris was putting beer in the fridge.

'What's up man,' I said. 'How was work.'

He opened a beer and offered me one and I said no and he somehow got into telling me how much he hated having sex with Victoria.

I was amazed at how he strung me up.

I could tell he'd been just waiting for an opportunity.

Victoria was really a prude or something and wouldn't let him fuck her from behind.

She was boring.

Other stuff.

He complained about her pussy hair being too long when they first met and said that he 'had to say something.'

'Man who gives a shit,' I said, laughing, walking away to use the bathroom.

He laughed like *b'HA*, then said 'Fuck you' as I closed the bathroom door.

*

After we ate, Chris and Victoria went out to the bar.

Robby and I sat in the lot, getting high.

He told me something had been different with Chris.

'Like since birth? Beginning of the bloodline?'

But Robby wasn't laughing, or even smiling.

Told me a couple nights when I hadn't been around, he and Chris had been fighting.

Like really fighting.

We'd always wrestled and shit, but now, Robby said, it was different.

'What do you mean?' I said.

'I don't know, man,' he said. It wasn't something he could define. 'I mean, I just put dumbass in a headlock and send him to bed, but, yenno,' Robby said, shrugging.

He took a pull off his smoke, eyeing me.

It was maybe the first time I'd noticed that his face looked aged.

'Let's just beat the shit out of him,' I said eventually, taking a joint out of my pocket.

Robby laughed. 'He's such a weasel. I don't know.'

'You give him too much slack,' I said.

'I know,' he said, hitting ash off his cigarette with his ring finger.

'Don't give him any slack,' I said.

'I know,' Robby said.

'Okay.'

And we sat in the mosquito-y darkness, alley light on trees, ground wet and cool, smell of smoke in the air.

I asked Robby how his dad was doing.

Talked about how his dad called us 'the stupids' growing up.

Childhood stories.

I had him laughing.

'I'm glad you're here, man,' Robby said, patting my shoulder as he got up to check the coals.

Then came Chris's hyena laugh, from somewhere down the alley.

'Buhhhh,' Robby said.

Victoria came around into the lot, her arms folded.

Chris was really drunk and laughing hysterically, following behind.

He'd slashed a bunch of tires on rental bikes, and broke the credit card terminal thing with a brick.

He always carried a steak knife around with him.

'Yeah it was awesome you guys,' Victoria said, making a face. 'You should've seen it.'

Chris laughed like a hyena and shook his head. 'I'm such an idiot,' he said. 'Fuckit though.'

Robby smiled and said, 'What the fuck?' gesturing with his hand in a half shrug. 'Just break shit here. Don't fucking get us all arrested. I have a job. I feed you.'

Chris laughed his hyena laugh and said, 'Man, fuck you, you're my lawyer.' Then he just sat there, extremely drunk and slouching in his chair, laughing, sometimes tonelessly repeating rap lyrics.

Nobody said anything.

Bathing in the smoky darkness.

Robby got up to check the coals again.

Victoria smoked a cigarette, staring at the ground.

Her bottom row of teeth shuddered, one sleeve hanging limp, arm inside against her body.

It was quiet, except for some kids yelling down the block.

Chris stood, hiking up his pants.

He grabbed the football and slapped it against his hand a few times. 'Yo, Rob,' he said.

'I'm good man, not now,' Robby said. 'I can't see shit.'

He was really drunk too.

Sleepy-looking, slouching back into the lawn chair and pinching his bottom lip.

'Come on, don't be a bitch,' said Chris. 'Come on.'

He slapped the football a few more times, held it back as if about to pass.

'I'm good,' Robby said again, getting out another cigarette and smiling. 'I'm where I want to be heh heh.'

Chris stared for a second, wobbling.

His smile turned into a weird look.

Like when you forget what you were laughing at.

He stood there staring, gripping and regripping the football.

Wobbling.

He laughed his hyena laugh and leaned back.

'Fuck you then, bitch,' he said, throwing the football.

It hit the apartment building, barely missing Robby.

Donk.

'Fucking quit it man,' Robby said, shrugging. 'I just fucking told you.'

Robby's eyes were open now.

Wide and buzzing.

Chris picked up a bottle. 'Come on man, I'll throw this up, you hit it with the football.'

'Babe, just sit down,' Victoria said.

'I said I'm good man,' Robby said. 'Fucking quit it. You're pissing me off.'

'Yeah Rob?'

Chris stood there wobbling.

He gnashed his teeth, bug-eyed.

'Please, just sit down,' Victoria said.

But Chris said, 'Fuck you,' and threw the bottle.

Robby blocked it and it broke against the ground.

'Stop,' said Victoria loudly.

I went to tackle Chris but he ran at Robby.

They collided.

The lawn chair tipped and they went down.

'I told you to *fucking stop*,' Robby yelled, landing on Chris and punching him twice in the back of the head.

Vunk vunk.

'Stop, ahhhh stop,' Chris said. 'Ahhhh.' He got up slowly, holding his hand, dirt on his face. 'Fuck guys. I'mmmm fucked . . .'

There was blood all over, flowing from between his fingers and down his arms as he clutched the wound.

Lots of blood.

Like his hand was pissing.

He'd landed in broken glass.

'Fuck,' he said.

Then he hurried inside, off-balance.

We followed.

'Jesus,' said Robby.

Victoria remained in her lawn chair, twitching the leg she had crossed over the other.

There was blood all over the dirt, the dead leaves, the walking stones, up the moldy back stairway.

Blood all over the kitchen floor.

Chris had a horrible wound between his fingers.

It pumped blood into the sink as he winced and said 'fuck' over and over.

'I'm fugggged.'

His eyes were red and teary.

He tried putting a cigarette in his mouth from the pack with one hand.

Bleeding everywhere.

Robby said we should go to the hospital.

Chris laughed. 'I can't afford the fucking *hospital*. Are you fuckin retarded?' Blood poured from his hand. 'Shiiiiiiiid,' he said, wincing.

Robby insisted, saying he'd pay for it. 'Come on man, that's nasty.'

He lit Chris's cigarette.

'What don't you fuckin get, man?' said Chris, taking a drag off his cigarette, slowly moving his fingers beneath the faucet. 'I can't fuckin *go to the hospital*. I can't even fuckin work now.'

There was blood on his shirt.

Blood in the sink.

Blood all over the white floor, mixing with dirt.

'Fuck,' he said, slowly moving the fingers. 'Ahhh.'

It was more of a trench than a cut, so we couldn't even sew it up.

Could barely get a look as it pumped.

Robby made a giant wad of folded paper towel and poured vodka on it and pressed it into the wound and wrapped duct tape around it.

Chris moaned, like *Dddduhhhh*.

There was blood all over both of them when it was done.

But it worked.

It contained the blood.

Victoria came in, arms folded. 'Are you all right?' she mumbled, looking at the bloody floor.

Chris laughed his hyena laugh. 'Yeah, I'm fucking *all right*. Thanks.'

He stared at her bug-eyed, wobbling in place.

Looking like he was trying to bite his own teeth.

'Hey settle the fuck down man,' I said. 'The fuck is wrong with you.'

We looked at each other.

I remembered him trying to fight me at a party years earlier and I'd just thrown him down and put him in a headlock and leaned on him while he screamed.

He had the same look in his eyes tonight.

It looked like another him was trying to tear through the original him.

He looked at his hand and, in a softer tone, said, 'I'm fugggged.'

We went and sat in the living room.

Robby and Chris chain-smoked, covered in blood.

Victoria touched her side ponytail, staring vaguely at the trash-covered coffee table.

Chris repeatedly explained how fucked he was.

Some sickness you can get from cleaning an aquarium with an open wound.

It sounded impressive and scary.

Except people like him always end up fine.

'I'm sure you'll be fine,' I said, looking at him and smiling.

And we looked at each other for another long moment before he looked away.

He laughed through his nose, taking a drag off the cigarette and shaking his head.

Everyone was quiet.

The wind blew outside.

*

When winter came, we were inside more.

Nothing but small golden Christmas lights and snow and gray outside.

Freezing temperatures.

Nothing to do.

And Chris was unbearable.

Robby was right.

Something about him had changed.

I'd never really liked him.

But this was different.

He broke up with Victoria.

Got jumped and beaten by some gangbangers for talking shit while drunk.

Doing more coke.

Always broke.

So I spent more time with a girl I'd been seeing.

But then, after being gone for a week one time, Robby messaged me.

He asked me to meet him downtown at his office, maybe get a drink or dinner.

So I walked downtown.

At dinner, he told me we were being evicted.

At first I was confused.

But then I didn't care.

Felt like I already knew.

Chris hadn't been paying rent for a while and Robby'd covered it initially, but now . . .

And more importantly, could I just stay at the place tonight?

'Somebody else has to be there, man,' he said.

We went home.

*

Chris was sitting on the couch in the dark, doing coke out of the Frisbee.

He was wearing his coat and winter hat, watching the Olympics.

'Heat's busted again,' he said, laughing his hyena laugh as we walked in.

The apartment smelled like jelly bean puke, beer, and smoke.

I sat down, keeping my jacket on. 'Fuck,' I said, rubbing my hands.

'Yup,' said Robby.

'Oh, hey Slim C!' I said to the kitten at my feet.

Slim Charles was a kitten Chris had adopted from an aquarium-cleaning client.

Chris hated the kitten because his tail was crooked.

Slim Charles climbed up my pants, then climbed my arm and perched on my shoulder, like a parrot.

He sniffed my ear, then sneezed into it.

I turned my hood sideways to cover him.

He lay there purring.

Chris was doing the lip-licking thing that meant he'd done too much coke.

Which was any amount.

It looked like his head was trying to shit out his eyes.

Sitting there on the couch, the blue light of some snowy event coming back at his face.

'Who's winning the Olympics?' I said, smiling.

Robby laughed and said, 'Yeah.'

Chris turned and looked at me, then Robby.

He didn't say anything, just stared at Robby, grinding his teeth.

'What's up, is there a fucking problem?' Robby said, leaning forward and clasping his hands.

Chris looked at the coffee table, smiling. 'Rob,' he said. 'Rob.'

He laughed his hyena laugh, shaking his head and smiling, eyes watering.

'So, how many holes should we put in the walls before we leave?' I said.

But Chris picked up a wrench from the coffee table and looked at Robby. 'My problem is that you won't shut the fuck up, you cunt.'

I couldn't tell if he was joking.

Robby smiled and said, 'Yeah because I'm the reason we're getting evicted, you piece of shit. I'm the cunt.'

Chris stood up, held the wrench high, laughing and licking his lips. 'Shut the fuck up. I'm gonna kill you motherfucker,' he said, skinny knuckles pulsing with the grip. He didn't blink, just wobbled, grinding his teeth. 'I'm gonna kill you, Rob,' he said quietly. 'I'm gonna smash your fucking face in, you rich piece of shit.'

He laughed his hyena laugh.

Nobody said anything.

Nobody moved.

Except for Chris, wobbling and biting at his lips.

A bobblehead with questionable autonomy.

'I'm gonna fuckin kill you, Rob,' he said.

'Okay fine kill me, just shut the fuck up and sit down. I'm sick of this shit. I paid your fucking rent and you treat me like this? *Fuck you, man.*'

'Yeah, get the fuck out of here,' I said.

Chris didn't say anything for a second, just eyed Robby and me back and forth, grinding his teeth.

He looked scared.

But then he smiled.

He leaned back like he was gonna throw the wrench, laughing. 'Here it comes, Rob. Here it coooooooomes.'

Robby said, 'I bet you won't.'

Everything was tense.

Then Chris threw his arm forward, but held on to the wrench.

And Robby flinched, then yelled, 'Fucking IT,' grabbing Chris's hand and tackling him onto the couch. They wrestled and then Robby put him in a choke hold. 'I told you to fucking stop!' He leaned back and yanked Chris's neck.

Chris dropped the wrench and grabbed at Robby's arms.

He sprawled his legs out, kicking shit off the coffee table.

He snorted terribly, choking like *eggghhhhhckkkkk*, eyes bulging.

Robby squeezed hard. 'Fucking stop,' he yelled again, then let go.

Chris fell to the ground, breathing heavily, knocking empty cans around.

Holding his neck.

Shirt and hair all messed up.

He struggled to breathe.

'I fucking told you, you piece of shit,' Robby said, breathing hard as well. He was pointing at Chris's face. 'I told you, motherfucker.'

'I'm gonna fucking, *kill you*, Rob,' Chris said again, weakly, with script-like insistence. He looked up at Rob, still holding his neck. 'I'm gonna fucking *kill you*.'

'If you come near me again I'll kill YOU. I'm done with your bullshit. Promise.'

Chris grabbed the wrench off the ground and stumbled outside, leaving the front door open.

A cold gust went up my pant leg.

Wind and snowflakes blew into the apartment.

Slim Charles hid behind the TV.

'Fuck is that asshole *doing*,' Robby said, lighting a cigarette with shaky hands. 'We just, we gotta get out, man. I'm sorry. I'm fucking sorry.'

Then there was a cracking sound and some laughter.

Another cracking sound.

Another.

Chris came back in laughing.

He sat on the couch holding his stomach, wrench in hand.

'I fucked up someone's windshield, buh HA.'

I looked outside.

A car parked directly out front of our building had the windshield caved and spidered in three spots.

Chris laughed hard, holding his stomach, wrench still in hand.

The veins in his neck filled with mounds.

He got up and looked out the doorway, up and down the block.

Standing in the doorway holding the wrench up, cigarette in his other hand.

He wobbled in place against the moonglow.

He took a drag off his cigarette, smoke blowing back into the apartment.

He went outside.

There was another cracking sound.

Then another.

Robby and I went out the back door and down the alley to go to a bar and avoid the cops if they came.

'I'm moving out tomorrow man, I'm sorry,' said Robby. 'I'm really sorry, man. But I mean, shit.'

*

After we got evicted, none of us really talked.

Robby got his own place, Chris found his way back in with Victoria, and I moved in with the girl I was seeing.

I saw Victoria briefly, when I went to her bakery to drop off some of her books.

I set the books down on the counter and she smiled at me and waved, helping a customer.

And that was it.

*

A couple months later, Robby emailed me.

The subject line read: 'Hey man, you need to read this.'

Inside the email was a link.

The link took me to a crime report page for Humboldt Park.

It listed the mugshots of four murder suspects from the weekend.

The first three were gang related.

The fourth was Chris.

He'd strangled Victoria.

*

I didn't really see Robby for a while after that.

Didn't have a chance to discuss it with him.

He was busy with work and his girlfriend.

Plus I figured he didn't want to talk.

There was something cold between us.

An ugly feeling.

One night, I texted him: 'Paging the saucemaster . . .'

'Haha what's up, shithead,' he replied.

And he invited me over.

He was engaged now.

I met his fiancée and saw their new place.

It was clean.

Looked like a place where humans lived.

He even had a new grilling setup in the backyard.

'Finally,' he said, slapping my shoulder, 'a reason to go through the rest of that bag of three hundred mini hotdogs!'

His fiancée shook her head and explained they'd taken a tour of a Vienna beef factory, where Robby had bought a bag of three hundred mini hotdogs.

So we sat in his backyard getting high and eating mini hotdogs.

We told his fiancée stories about growing up.

About how our only entertainment was throwing rocks at each other.

About fights in the alley.

We said retroactive condolences for pets that'd died.

Discussed classmates' fates.

Family shit.

When it got dark, we went inside and sat at the kitchen table.

Robby's fiancée lit a candle and dimmed the lights and said she was going to bed.

We hugged.

I said it was nice to meet her.

Robby and I stayed up, drinking red wine and getting high.

We recounted more childhood stories.

Condolences for grandmas we didn't know had passed.

I reminded him that I'd sometimes cut his grandma's grass and she'd paid me in sandwiches.

He laughed and said, 'Oh sweet Nana. She really loved you.'

A cat walked up to my leg and headbutted me.

'Slim C!' I said, picking up Slim Charles, who Robby had taken in and was now fully grown.

Slim C put the side of his head against my chest and purred.

I asked about Chris. 'What's going on with him?' I said. 'We never really talked.'

Robby raised his eyebrows and breathed out.

He recapped the night.

Chris and Victoria were still living together, but hadn't been dating, or whatever.

Chris called Robby and told him things weren't going well.

He and Victoria were arguing, and he didn't know what to do.

Said it was bad.

So Robby told him to come over and stay with him instead.

But Chris declined.

Robby told him to relax and they'd talk tomorrow.

'You know how he gets when he's fucked up,' Robby said. 'Like a goofy squirrel or raccoon or some shit.'

But then Chris called back a couple hours later and just said, 'She's dead,' when Robby answered.

So Robby went to Victoria's apartment.

Chris was already out front.

He'd called the police on himself.

'I don't know man,' said Robby, taking a sip of wine. 'Something was up with him, man. I'm not making excuses I mean, he's a piece of shit, I hope he fucking dies, but I'm just saying, he was so fucked up he looked like an animal or something, I don't know. He looked like a fucking weasel or rat. I'm serious man. Like he was morphing. I couldn't understand anything he was saying.'

The police showed up and took them both in.

Robby was detained for twelve hours.

The coroner said she'd been dead for hours by the time the police arrived.

Which—Robby said, tears forming in his eyes—meant Victoria was probably dead the first time Chris called that night.

We were quiet.

In the candlelight.

'Stupid guy Slim Charles was there too,' said Robby, nodding toward my lap. 'Poor little guy was in the bathtub shivering the next day when we remembered him.'

Tears fell down Robby's face.

He blinked a couple times.

Said Chris had broken his thumb strangling her.

'Fuck man,' I said, closing my eyes.

We sat there in silence.

Robby said that Chris and Victoria were arguing about Victoria sleeping with someone else, even though they weren't dating at the time and he'd slept with other people, open relationship whatever.

'You should've seen this kid too,' Robby said, smiling, arms folded. Tears filled his eyes again, talking about the guy. 'I know this guy. I've seen him around. This guy's a fucking, he's a little dweeb, you know?' He smiled, and a tear went down his face as he shrugged.

He did an impression of the dweeb kid.

It consisted of him hunching over and going, *hern hern* in a nasally voice, front teeth over his bottom lip.

And for some reason, it comforted me.

Not the impression of the dweeb, but the idea of Victoria having sex with this dweeb.

Not the idea of Victoria having sex with the dweeb, but doing anything, at the same time as all the rest of us, doing whatever.

No real fate.

The idea of doing anything.

The possibility of doing things.

The greatness of anything, through living eyes.

The way if you were stranded in the desert, you would feel like a candy bar was the greatest thing.

Or deep in outer space you'd think a sidewalk was amazing.

The way anything could be that way if you just focused and understood.

Breaking bottles in a backyard.

Talking about books.

Robby and I sat in the candlelight, silently drinking.

Slim Charles slept in my lap, swishing his tail.

Robby told me he'd talked to Chris a few times on the phone.

Chris was making friends in jail and playing a lot of chess.

He'd recently been sentenced to fifteen years in prison, to be transferred downstate soon.

Said he had no idea why he did what he did and looks back on himself as a completely different person since sobering up.

'Fuck him,' I said.

Robby's eyes were glassy.

Slim Charles swished his tail lightly in my lap.

We were quiet for a while.

Robby poured us both another glass of wine and tossed me a bag of weed to roll a joint.

I started to feel dizzy.

Horrible images came to me involuntarily.

Victoria, rotten, floating into space, then opening her eyes and swimming away, hair flowing as if underwater.

Passing away.

Her pale body, eyes closed, floating to the bottom of a dark ocean.

Sinking in mud.

Robby said some things about feeling guilty.

He was crying again and looked small and defeated.

Like there was a series of events he could've directed, that would've ended otherwise.

Like he wasn't him, and Chris wasn't himself, and I wasn't me, and everything else wasn't everything else.

Like it was all up to him.

Tears ran down his face.

He cleared his throat.

'Anyhow,' he said, then thanked me for vague reasons. He put his hand on mine and slapped it a few times, his voice wavering. 'It's great to see you, man. It really is.'

He cleared his throat again.

'Yeah man,' I said.

We each took a drink of our wine and smoked the joint.

Robby said he was going to bed but that I should stay and sleep in their guest room.

I said thanks and good night and went to the guest room, shutting the door behind me and standing in the quiet.

I took off my clothes and got in bed, exhausted.

But when I closed my eyes, I began to see bad shit again.

Horrible things imported behind my eyes.

I saw bugs.

I saw skeletons floating into and out of different areas of darkness.

I saw blood.

There were awful sounds.

Sneering, bloody teeth.

People screaming.

Moonlight on a bruised neck.

Victoria on her back, naked and blue, arrows traveling through her in different directions, like how they depict wind on a weather forecast.

Passing.

Eyes closing.

Flies on her face.

Marks all over her neck.

Body turning to ash.

Dead.

I turned and lay on my stomach, facedown in the pillow, arms folded beneath.

Muddy teeth grinding.

Lifeless eyes.

Shrieking bugs in darkness.

Gray skin.

Eye veins turning black.

Lights going out in faraway houses.

A forest of leafless trees.

Victoria throws a bottle into the air and it turns to wasps.

I was biting down hard and felt sick.

Gripped.

Dizzy.

And then it broke, soaking me in cold sweat.

And I saw Victoria—her face blue, eyes closed—sinking to the bottom of the ocean.

Hitting the ocean floor quietly as her hair catches up to her.

Then not moving.

Everything darkening around her.

Everything going dark.

But then—a light, beginning from her chest and expanding outward, absorbing all shapes and contours, all things.

Total and blinding.

And as it clears, we're back in the kitchen at the old apartment, next to the empty lot.

On a warm summer night.

With hours ahead of us.

And no real fate.

Something cooking outside.

Robby and Chris throwing the football at a broken door.

Victoria and I talking about books.

And she smiles, looking downward.

'Look alive,' Chris says, laughing, as the football flies into the kitchen and knocks empty cans and bottles off the counter.

Jumping Rope

I had a jump rope I took from the high school where my ex worked.

So I started jumping rope whenever I had nothing to do.

It was my antidote.

Jumping rope.

That would be my saving.

Anytime I felt bad, or had too much time, I'd go to the alley and jump rope.

There.

Easy.

If I was jumping rope, then I'd be jumping rope, and nothing else could be happening.

Hard to worry about anything if you had to keep jumping over a rope.

Today, when I went out to the alley, there was an older lady in multiple bathrobes and something wrapped around her head, pushing a steel shopping cart and looking through dumpsters.

She came up and stopped her cart by me.

We smiled at each other and said hello and she started going through the dumpster.

I started jumping rope.

Felt like I had to put on a show.

I had an audience, even though she wasn't even looking.

So I did a few high jumps, bringing my knees all the way up to my chest, slapping the rope down twice before landing.

Couple of crisscrosses—you know, the usual.

Then I got into a steady groove.

I cruised for a while.

Jumping just high enough to avoid the rope.

My heart beat hard but I breathed slowly to calm it.

It was a trick I learned—not to focus on legs, but your heart.

Heart, the motor.

Heart, the key.

The lady continued picking through the trash, accepting some items, refusing others, checking stuff already in her cart, and so on.

Seemed like quite a process.

I kept thinking she was going to leave, but she didn't.

My legs started to burn.

Throat felt thick and hot.

I was ready to stop.

But then I started silently cheering on my heart.

Go, little heart, go.

Goddamnit, keep going.

I'm not sure how much time passed, but I kept jumping.

I had to last.

It meant something.

One legged.

Then the other leg.

Switching legs, running, whipping the rope side to side without jumping, back to jumping, couple more high jumps, et cetera.

Sweating insanely.

Mouth dry.

Blood flushing through my burning legs.

I ached.

Eventually, the lady closed the dumpster lid and secured her cart again, tossing a tarp over everything.

I landed on both feet, put my hands on my hips breathing hard.

Felt like someone had crushed my legs, but in a sexual way.

They twitched.

The lady smiled at me and began pushing her cart, crunching and creaking over rocks.

'Thank you for performing for me,' she said as she passed.

'You're welcome,' I said.

She went down the alley as I limped to the fire escape and crawled up.

The Sandwich Maker

The sandwich maker hates you too.

He walks through a door into the kitchen area of a bar/restaurant in Lincoln Park and clocks in on a computer.

It's the weekend.

'Gentlemen,' he says to the cook and the dishwasher.

Yes, the sandwich maker hates you and anyone that can be even vaguely associated with you.

He hates you as his duty—second only to making sandwiches.

Because these are your sandwiches.

Your mess.

You and anyone related to you by birth, your extended family, extended family's friends, schoolmates, dentist, et al., fuck it, anyone you've in any way interacted with at all.

He finishes buttoning his work shirt over a dago tee, idly checking the sandwich station to see if anything needed to be sliced or re-filled or whatever, fuck.

A shift's beginning.

One of the worst feelings.

Peacefully surrendering to the mess.

'I'm not going to do shit today,' he says.

'Thass right!' yells the cook, snapping his tongs.

'Fuck off, Homer,' says the sandwich maker.

But then the cook extends his tongs underneath the heat lamp.

And the sandwich maker reaches his hand underneath the heat lamp, forefinger extended for the cook to gently pinch.

'Yes, my son, yes,' says the cook.

A ticket prints on a machine near the heat lamp.

'Into the shit, gentlemen,' says the sandwich maker, taking the ticket and pinning it on a track above the expo counter.

The orders.

The tickets.

Sandwich after bullshit fucking sandwich.

Standing in front of the station for hours.

Hours and hours.

The same fucking sandwiches every night.

Different asshole customers, same fucking sandwiches.

Fuck.

A server comes into the kitchen and leans against the handwashing sink, texting.

She says, 'Ew it smells in here. You guys smell that? It's like someone ate a fart then puked it back up.'

She's laughing before she even finishes and then everyone else laughs too.

'Goddamn,' says the dishwasher, wiping his eye.

'Turkey pesto!' yells the cook, tearing off another ticket from the machine.

The sandwich maker takes out two slices of bread from a bag.

Fuck.

He makes between thirty and forty fucking turkey pesto sandwiches a night, and that's not including the other sandwiches.

He brushes butter/garlic mixture onto each slice then puts them on a panini press, lowering the top.

He presses the top down and it makes a sound like *tisssss*.

'Diiiieee,' he says, smiling.

The server says, 'Burn, die, you son of a bitch,' typing an order into the computer.

The sandwich maker grabs a mixing bowl.

He fills it with ingredients from the sandwich station.

Turkey.

Arugula.

Red onion.

Poached cherry tomatoes.

Fresh mozzarella.

Pesto.

Plus all of the hate, poison, and death he can transmit through his hands, eyes, and heart.

Please—please feel my hate, he thinks.

He moves the ingredients around in the bowl.

Fingering the cold bullshit.

Not wearing gloves.

He never wears gloves.

'Hey, put some gloves on, fuckface,' says the chef, coming up from downstairs holding a bunch of ingredients.

The chef.

The chef doesn't hate anyone.

Because he hates everything.

There's nothing personal about it.

He hates people, of course, so like, you too, sure, but also rocks, trees, birds, ideas, whatever.

This afternoon he's so hungover and baggy eyed and haggard it's like a genetic reversion.

'You look like ten pounds of shit in a five-pound bag, BWAH,' says the cook.

'Fuck you, Homer,' says the chef. 'Just, die.'

And he stands at the expo counter for a second and closes his eyes, tapping the cutting board with his knuckles.

He opens his eyes.

'Gloves, gloves,' he says, whipping the sandwich maker with a hand towel.

Fwick.

The towel snaps against the sandwich maker's arm.

'No, fuck you,' says the sandwich maker, snatching the towel away, then handing it back. 'I never wear gloves.'

The chef considers it for a moment, then nods. 'All right cool,' he says, shrugging and laughing hoarsely. 'What am I gonna do. I need the fucking sandwich.'

'Exactly,' says the sandwich maker. 'I'll seriously never wear gloves. I'll quit. I'll walk out. You can fire me. Whatever. I'm not wearing gloves. There's nothing you can do.'

'Tellem,' yells the cook, wiping sweat off his head.

The chef raises his hands, shrugging a little. 'Okay. Hey, look . . . that's okay.'

He grabs some cheap promotional sunglasses from a tequila company off the ticket counter and puts them on to help with his hangover.

The sandwich maker takes the bread off the press, burning his fingers.

'Goddamnit,' he says, throwing the bread down onto the long cutting board in front of the sandwich station. He dumps the ingredients from the bowl to the bread. 'I hope whoever eats this chokes on it, then falls and hits their head on the floor and dies.'

The chef hunches over, laughing and coughing.

'You like that, huh?' says the sandwich maker, smiling.

The chef shakes his head, coughing. 'No. You have, the worst fucking attitude of any human I've ever encountered. Even the rats in the alley care more about their species. It's actually impressive.' He coughs terribly into his hand, adjusts the sunglasses.

The sandwich maker cuts the sandwich in half diagonally, using a seesaw motion and both hands, to avoid compressing it.

He wraps the sandwich halves with red and white checkered wax paper.

'Holy fuck,' says the chef, punching the sandwich maker on the shoulder. 'Look at that wrap.'

The sandwich maker smiles and winks.

'You go, babyboy,' yells the server, putting her notepad into her apron then typing an order into the computer.

'Hell of a wrap,' says the chef, tossing a handful of chips onto the plate, then waving dismissively. 'Now get it out of my face.'

A server takes it away.

The cook says, 'Take them sunglasses off, nigga. Broke-ass Elvis-looking muthafucka.'

'Make some fucking wings, Homer, or I'll come back there and cut your fat-baby head off.'

The cook laughs a high-pitched laugh and stomps the floor, clacking the tongs. He points his tongs at the chef under the heat lamp and says, 'This motherfucker got jokes.'

A ringing sound comes out of a small electronic device hanging near the ticket printer.

It's a device connected to an ordering service that delivers food for people who want food from a place that doesn't deliver.

The sandwich maker says, 'I'm putting razors and a fucking bomb in this order.' He reads the ticket. 'All right, Kenneth Hurley, I'm coming for you. Here I come. You wanted a fucking sandwich, well now you're gonna fucking die.'

The cook wipes his forehead and drops some wings into the fryer, yelling, 'Die motherfucker *die!*'

'Shut up and just make the sandwich,' says the chef, putting a cigarette in his mouth. 'I'm going outside for a sec.'

The sandwich maker puts a sandwich on a plate and tosses the plate onto the ticket counter.

Clang.

He scrapes off the panini press with a bent-up, grease-caked grill brush.

'The fuck do we still have this?' he says to himself.

The brush is absurd.

It barely exists in any recognizable form.

Like an abomination that crawled out of a tar pit.

The tickets begin to print more rapidly.

Bigger orders.

More specifications.

Corrections.

Table changes.

Sides.

Carryout orders.

Ordering device ringing nonstop.

Another sandwich maker clocks in and mumbles hi to everyone, buttoning up his shirt.

The senior sandwich maker.

Used to be a Hell's Angel.

He has tattoos of devils and shit all over his arms and a big beard, in which he keeps the broken end of a plastic fork, for grooming.

He and the other sandwich maker bump fists, then stand side by side, making sandwiches.

The sandwich station: their palette.

The ingredients: their paint.

The thankless faces of the neighborhood: their canvas.

'Kill everyone,' says the Hell's Angel, staring at the ingredients.

'Turkey pesto!' yells the cook, tearing off the ticket with his tongs. 'That's for you, sweetie.'

'Man,' says the Hell's Angel, pausing to comb his beard with the broken plastic fork. 'I fucking dream about making these moth-erfuckers. I hear phantom ringing for to-go orders.'

He tugs at his beard with the fork, making a sound like *tzick tzick*.

'Shit man,' says the sandwich maker. 'You should probably kill yourself. I mean if I dreamt about that, I'd kill myself the second I woke up.'

The Hell's Angel laughs and wraps up a sandwich. 'Hey, hand me that tape.'

'It's right in front of you.'

'Oh shit,' says the Hells Angel, laughing. 'Sorry, I'm fuckin blind.' He squints his one eye a little. 'I got a fucked-up eye.'

'What happened?'

'Got into a car accident and smashed it on the steering wheel. Peeled back my whole eyelid. I could see with it closed.'

'Fuuuuuck,' says the cook as he eats a chicken wing.

'That's fucked up.'

The Hell's Angel takes out a big container of shredded lettuce from beneath the sandwich station and puts more lettuce into a smaller container. 'Man, it was like some nightmare shit. I'm at the ER and they're sewing it up and I can see the shit the whole time. Fucking needle coming right at my eye, over and over.'

'There's a needle in my eye dude!' says the cook in a California-surfer accent.

More tickets print.

The dinner rush.

Cook swearing.

Dishwasher swearing.

Servers complaining.

Chef whipping everyone with his hand towel.

Fwick fwick.

The sandwich makers stand there, making the same six sand-wiches, sometimes with extra whatever, or no whatever, or a side of whatever, or whatever whatever.

Sandwich after sandwich.

Toasting bread, throwing ingredients into a mixing bowl, lay-ering cold cuts, spraying on condiments, assembling, cutting, wrapping, staring off, dying.

The same process.

Different ingredients.

No end.

'Hey, I'm just gonna say this,' says the sandwich maker, 'but if you order anything from here, I don't care if it's the simplest order or whatever, but I fuckin hate you. I automatically hate you.' He shrugs, holding a giant knife. 'That's it.' He cuts a sandwich in half. 'And that goes for you too'—he checks the ticket—'Dorothy Wayne. You're next.' He scratches his beard with the blunt side of the knife.

A server rolling silverware stops and makes a disgusted face. 'Everyone except me is so gross here, seriously. I bet your beard smells worse than his,' she says, nodding toward the Hell's Angel.

The Hell's Angel laughs and shakes his head.

He picks at his beard with the broken plastic fork.

'No I'm serious,' says the server, doing a motion as if zipping air together sideways. 'All of you should be in prison.' Then she smiles and clasps her hands over her chest. 'Unless one of you gets me that side of green ranch I asked for.'

The Hell's Angel smiles, putting mayo on a sandwich. 'I already been to prison, ma. You go there, you come back and be a nice little sandwich-monkey like me.' He taps the clogged mayo bottle on the cutting board. 'Having dudes jerk off while you're trying to take a shit . . . fuck that.'

The sandwich maker says, 'I feel like I wouldn't want someone jerking off while I'm shitting, but I wouldn't want to be told not to jerk off while someone else is shitting, if that makes sense.'

The cook says, 'You get your ass beat?'

The Hell's Angel says, 'Dude, first week I's in, they take all the new people into the bathroom two at a time to fight someone who's been in for a while. I had to fight this fucking huge-ass dude. Guy was totally ripped and greased up and ready to fuckin kill me.' He cuts a sandwich in half and puts the knife next to it to keep it from falling over. 'They send us into the shower area and I'm fuckin—I mean I ain't no bitch—but I's worried.' He tears off some wrapping paper. 'So we go into the shower area and I'm like, fuck. This guy looked like he was gonna destroy me, but I at least wanted to hurt him somehow. You gotta makem pay. So this motherfucker comes rushing at me and I just moved a little and my fuckin hand, like'—he does a motion as if about to fall off a skateboard—'slipped off his head and he lost his balance and fell, busted his face on the ground, knocked himself the fuck out.'

'Oh shit,' says the sandwich maker, laughing.

The Hell's Angel nods. 'Me and him walk back out a half minute later, him lumped up and confused and me totally fine. Nobody fucked with me after that.' He laughs.

'Haha you lucky bitch!' yells the cook, pointing with his tongs. 'I'dve fucked you up.'

The Hell's Angel smiles as he finishes the wrap.

'Supposed to be no vinaigrette on that boss,' says the chef, coming back in, checking the tickets.

The Hell's Angel says, 'Goddamnit,' and throws the sandwich against the ground.

Fwump.

The server laughs. 'The sound that made was hilarious.'

And the dinner rush continues.

Tickets.

Orders.

Tables.

Orders.

Tickets.

Sandwiches.

Tickets.

Tables.

The mess.

Eventually, there's a lull.

And the sandwich maker wipes down the deli slicer, knocking small shreds/paste/lumps of different deli meats—in various stages of dehydration—onto the floor.

A server, cashing out nearby, yells, 'Ahhhh ahhhhhh, fuckkkkkk,' dancing around a little and holding her arm out.

There's a white, fatty paste stuck to her.

'Ew fuck!' she yells. 'What is that? Get it off get it off!'

She retches a few times.

Everyone laughs.

The server flicks it off her arm and it sticks to the area the sandwich maker just cleaned.

The sandwich maker says, 'I have to take a shit,' and goes downstairs.

He passes the Hell's Angel, who is on his way up the stairs from having just taken a shit.

The staff bathroom is a special place.

A sanctuary.

The sandwich maker sits on the toilet and shits.

Sweat runs down his neck into his chest hair.

Feet aching.

Vaguely pissed off.

But, for a second, transported.

Away.

Gone.

Somewhere else.

Surveying the clouds above during a beautiful sunset, on a planet all his own.

Inhaling the neon clouds as he passes, blowing them out as rainbows.

Happy.

Removed.

And when he opens his eyes, he notices a roach near his foot.

The roach is very still, on its back.

Then, a slight movement in one of its legs.

A dying twitch.

Like waving goodbye.

'Yikes!' says the sandwich maker, sitting there sweating.

He wipes his ass and flushes.

Takes a deep breath and exits the bathroom, returning to the mess.

Back upstairs, it's time to take out the garbage.

He grabs the giant trash can situated where the dishwasher works.

Every night it's full of the worst shit.

Just a giant, heavy, dripping, greasy bag of terrible shit.

Like if Santa were evil.

The sandwich maker rolls the can away and the Hell's Angel joins him and they go to the back door.

'Ready?' says the Hell's Angel.

The sandwich maker nods solemnly.

The Hell's Angel kicks the back door open hard.

A shitload of rats run by the doorway.

'Fuuuuuuck,' says the Hell's Angel, shaking his head.

He shivers.

He taps the dumpster with a broom handle.

More rats eek out from under the lid of the dumpster and fall to the ground, running away.

'I swear, sometimes when I'm out here alone, they do some mind-reading shit,' says the Hell's Angel, combing his beard with the broken plastic fork.

'You're just weak,' says the sandwich maker.

He unchains the second dumpster lid and opens it up and there's a huge rat sitting atop the garbage, eating something, looking stunned to have been discovered.

HUH?!!?!?

'Oh shit!' says the Hell's Angel.

The rat pauses, then leaps out of the dumpster and lands hard on the pavement by the Hell's Angel's feet.

He screams as the rat scrambles and runs away.

Then he's hunched over with one hand on his knee and the other over his heart, breathing hard.

'You fucking punk,' says the sandwich maker.

'Dude, he tried to bite my dick off.'

They lift the garbage can and dump the bag into the dumpster.

'Oh hey,' says the Hell's Angel, '[Chef] said something about a dead one by the back door here.'

'What, where?'

'Right by the back door. He wants you to clean it up. I'll show you.'

They look by the gangway.

The rat is on its side in a puddle, totally bloated.

'Holy fuck,' says the sandwich maker. 'Game over.' He makes the sign of the cross.

'Yeah,' says the Hell's Angel, '[Chef] said he wanted you to pick it up.'

'Yeah?'

'Yeah, he said you're the man for the job. Something about your elegant hands.'

'Ah.'

They go back inside.

The chef is dicing an onion on the sandwich line. 'One a you fucks get rid of that dead rat?'

'Yeah, I'm going to,' says the sandwich maker.

'Sounds good, big guy,' says the chef, wiping onion off the knife and eating a tiny cube.

'Can I use your knife to spear it and flip his ass into the dumpster?'

'How about some tongs, dipshit,' says the chef. He shrugs. 'Tongs?'

The sandwich maker grabs some tongs and goes toward the back door.

Outside, a light rain has begun.

The sandwich maker stands before the bloated rat corpse.

'Heavenly Rat Father,' he says. 'We ask not much of you, but that you guide our brother back to your kingdom. In peace I offer him up, amen.'

He leans over the handrail and holds on with one hand, balancing and grabbing the bloated rat corpse with the tongs.

'Therrrrrrre we go,' he says, righting himself back over the rail, groaning.

He holds the bloated rat corpse before him, watching water drip off its tail.

And something about it is so good.

Something only for him.

A moment of special joy.

He leans back with the tongs, then arches the rat far down the alley.

A wonderful toss.

Next he throws the tongs.

They land somewhere with a muted clank.

And he goes back inside.

Back into the mess.

The Hell's Angel is mixing turkey pesto ingredients in a bowl, swearing to himself.

The ordering device rings.

'Goddamnit,' says the sandwich maker. He scrolls through the order. 'Fries,' he says, looking around in horror. 'All they want is . . . fries . . . to go . . . This person ordered . . . fries to go.'

'Whuhhhhhhhhhh,' says the cook, looking stunned.

'*Fuck,*' whispers a server, putting her hand over her mouth.

For a moment, there they stand.

Stunned.

Immobilized by the horrors of a person morally exhausted enough to do such a thing.

Wishing that person, from their collective minds, in unison and with equal rage, a quick, brutal death at the hands of a reaper, who, raising its enormous blade, bellows, 'Fries to go?' before swinging downward.

The chef says, 'Cool, fine, fries to go. Just make them and shut the fuck up, cool?' Then he yells to the dishwasher. 'Hey stupid, lemme get some more ramekins.'

FLORIDA

Keeps You Sharp

This guy crossed paths with me walking through downtown St. Pete.

'Man, goddamnit,' he said, stopping by me, as though we'd already been talking.

So I stopped too.

'This motherfucker . . .' he said, gesturing out somewhere.

He had faded tattoos and big, raw pockmarks all over his forearms.

'I'm supposed to water these motherfuckin plants,' he said. 'But this asshole parked his car on my hose. I work over here, yenno?' He pointed somewhere. 'The guy who owns that building, he pays me to water the plants and then I clean the parking lot for the cops over there, yenno? But I go to get my hose today, boss says *hey you gotta water those plants* and I said *I'm chuh-RYin*, but this fucking car is parked on the hose and I couldn't get the hose out.'

'Shit,' I said.

He stood there shaking his head.

'Hey, nice ink,' he said, pointing to my arm. 'Who did that?'

'This guy in Chicago.'

'Oh I'm from Chicago too!' he said, backing up a little.

He held out his fist.

'Hell yeah,' I said.

We hit our fists together.

'Yeah I lived in Cicero, but I'd go downtown for drum lessons when I was a kid. I'm a drummer. Remember Franki Valenti's? That's where I took lessons. I'd take the train to Michigan Avenue and then walk to Wabash. I still play drums sometimes, over here,' he said, pointing somewhere.

'Nice. I play the drums too,' I said.

He leaned back. 'Yeah?'

'Yeah man.'

'So you know your paradiddles and shit then?'

'Yeah, for sure.'

'Okay let's see it,' he said, slapping a nearby concrete ledge.

I started slapping the ledge. 'Right-left-right-right, left-right-left-left,' I said.

'Hey, there you go,' he said, joining me.

We stood there doing paradiddles on the ledge.

Right-left-right-right.

Left-right-left-left.

Neither of us could really do them.

But pretty much.

Right-left-right-right.

Left-right-left-left.

'My teacher used to always tell me to practice my flams too,' he said. 'Always flams. I don't know why.'

He did some flams and choppy sixteenth notes, slapping them out on the concrete ledge.

'It keeps you sharp,' I said.

'Yeah for sure.' He slapped my elbow a little. 'Damn, you got some big-ass arms too.' He held up his arms. 'The military fucked up my arms. They shake too much now.'

I looked at the bloody holes on his arms.

'I like that tattoo,' I said, pointing to an eagle on his forearm.

It was an eagle with its wings spread, USA beneath.

'Yeah I got this one in the military and this one'—he held out his other pocked arm—'after Mom and Dad died.'

It was a crest.

He rolled up his T-shirt sleeve to show me the initials of his son in Old English font.

On his other bicep he had a small cartoon drawing of a boxer doing the 'dukes up' pose.

'Yeah I'm a boxer,' he said. 'I'm a big boxing guy.'

'Man, I love boxing,' I said, smiling.

'Yeah? I still box!' he said, pointing somewhere. 'I go over there. I love hitting motherfuckers in the face. I *love it*. I like getting hit too.' He shrugged. 'I don't know, I just like it. But yeah those are nice tattoos.'

'Where should I go around here to get tattooed? I've been looking for a place.'

'Oh, yeah,' he said, walking. 'Come on, I'll introduce you to the guys over here. Yeah I was supposed to water these fucking plants, yenno? I do it for this guy over there, he lets me water them and have a beer, he don't care.'

'That's cool.'

'I work for him and then the cops pay me to clean the parking lot. It keeps me out of trouble, yenno? But I can't get my fucking hose out from beneath this motherfucker's tire. This motherfucker parked his fucking car *right on the hose*. I'm pulling and pulling, nothing.'

'Fuck that guy,' I said. 'That's what I think.'

We walked down the block toward the tattoo place.

'It's that place right there,' he said. 'See the sign?'

There was a wooden, Western-style sign that said TATTOO hanging outside.

He led me into the shop.

'Hey Keller, hey Brian,' he said, 'think I brought you guys a new customer.'

The tattoo guys—one of them working on someone and the other going through a binder with someone—waved and said hi.

'This is the place to go,' said the guy who'd brought me, leaning on the counter. 'These guys are the best.'

I asked them for a business card.

The guy at the counter gave me one.

'All right thanks a lot, I'll come in sometime,' I said, waving to them.

Then I said thanks to the guy who'd brought me there.

'Have a good day, brother,' he said, holding out his hand.

We shook hands.

I went back outside into the heat and started walking.

Forgot which way was home.

So I just walked.

I tapped right-left-right-right, left-right-left-left on my thighs.

Right-left-right-right, left-right-left-left.

Then another one.

Then it got messed up and I started again.

Right-left-right-right.

Left-right-left-left.

I could still kind of do them.

The Ice Cream Man

I saw the ad in the jobs section of the newspaper while waiting to get my tires fixed.

WANTED: Ice Cream Truck Driver.

My calling had called.

And I—I called it back.

Somebody named Nicky answered and we set up an interview for the next day.

*

The office was in Clearwater.

I pulled off the highway and went down a road lined on either side by industrial buildings.

Tile places.

Paint places.

Pool cover places.

Motorcycles.

Et cetera.

Florida shit.

Everything broken, breaking, or being repaired.

The office was a squat, square concrete building next to a gravel lot, with a dozen or so ice cream trucks surrounded by a barbed wire fence.

Inside was one open room with coolers humming in rows under fluorescent lights.

Cold tombs.

I sat at a folding table with a sticky tablecloth, staring at the plastic flaps that led out back.

'Hi hullo, I'm Jerry,' said the old, overweight, bald man who let me in.

Nicky was more of the day-to-day boss, he explained.

Then he asked me a bunch of questions, the last of which was if I had any questions for him.

In my experience, that was a bad sign.

Like somebody coming out of a door, leaning back against the door and saying, 'Is there anything you'd like to know about what's behind the door?'

He took my driver's license to make a copy for a background check.

I sat there staring at the plastic flaps while he processed it.

The gravel lot.

The trucks.

The sun.

You work Wednesday through Sunday, twelve-hour days, Jerry said, handing me back my stuff.

The amount of money you make is up to you.

If you work hard, he said, holding up both hands, eyebrows raised, then you make more money.

He kept stressing how it'd be up to me.

I didn't like how that sounded either.

My whole life had been up to me and I was still only being considered for the position of ice cream man.

Fuck.

Jerry told me they don't pay until you've made three hundred dollars (like for your cut, which was 60 percent of daily sales) or two weeks went by.

So you got paid the amount up to three hundred dollars after two weeks, or three hundred dollars, whichever happened first.

Okay cool.

I mean, fuck, but fine.

'I'll coal you when the background check goes through,' Jerry said. 'Should be some time tamarra.'

Okay good.

Great.

Check my background, goddamnit.

See if I care.

We shook hands and I left.

*

My first day as an ice cream man I had to go in early for training, and the office was already busy.

Hoppin.

Movin.

The whole roster of ice cream men and one ice cream woman, all fifty to sixty plus years old, gathering ice cream sandwiches, popsicles, bomb pops, et cetera from various coolers, and tossing them into empty banana boxes.

Jerry had to do some final paperwork and then Nicky was going to train me on the truck and then, why then, I'd officially be an ice cream man.

I was already worried about running over a child.

Which was, basically, the remainder of Jerry's training.

How to not run over kids.

How to deal with people who might want to shoot you.

Things like that.

What it means to solicit in the state of Flarada.

My rights.

The rights of an ice cream man.

I even had to sign a three-year no-compete clause, guaranteeing I wouldn't work for another ice cream company in any of the same counties as them.

Jerry assured me that it wouldn't be lucrative to go into business on my own, either, since they bought 'three quartas of a million dollas a year' in ice cream.

Nicky arrived.

He wore basketball shorts, a black T-shirt like club security, and an all-black baseball hat, gold chain with crucifix on it.

He had the kind of physique that suggested lifting weights, but still very soft.

'Heyyyyy what's up,' he said, coming up and shaking my hand.

He walked me around the office.

They had maps all over.

Maps.

All of Tampa Bay and St. Petersburg.

With lines/areas drawn on them, names in the borders.

Highlighted.

Penned on.

Divided.

Strategized upon.

Scoured.

Seized and controlled.

Nicky showed me the general area I should stick to, citing not only our other drivers, but—as he explained with complete seriousness—another outfit, a private outfit, 'this Asian lady' who would 'literally run you off the road.'

I appreciated that type of commitment, and looked forward to my eventual test with her.

I would not disrespect or diminish her as an enemy, or laugh her off; I would embrace, confront, and destroy her.

We walked through the plastic flaps to the back lot.

I pictured myself accidentally running over kids, unable to stop.

Police trailing me, firing.

Bullets piercing the truck and killing me but I'm still running kids over until I hit a tree.

Blood all over the ice cream truck.

Fuck.

Nicky showed me the truck.

The sun was up and dumping its whitest light.

I sweated—squinting, feeling like shit.

Florida shit.

You take the cooler off the generator, hang the cord over here, plug the cooler into the inside battery, and you're good ta gaow.

He hung the extension cord over a particularly strong weed.

The job seemed easy.

The ice cream was in the cooler.

The cooler kept the ice cream cold.

Keep the ice cream cold.

Sell the ice cream.

Bring back the money.

Oh, and don't use the A/C because it'll drain the gas.

Fuuuhhhuuuuck.

Nicky pointed to a black box on the ceiling of the truck, just above the windshield.

There were two dials on it, one for the songs, and one for volume, and a switch in the middle.

'Flip this on, you're live. This one's fah volume. This one's the soangs. There's nine soangs, but you're gonna wanna keep it on Soang 7 the whole time. Other than that,' he said, turning the steering wheel side to side mindlessly, 'you're good ta gaow.'

Song 7 was a sine-wave instrumental of "Do Your Ears Hang Low?"

'Soang 7, volume up, just cruise, good ta gaow.'

I nodded.

Knowing that, though there were eight other songs, I would not listen to any of them—not a one, not for a second.

Many might be tempted to sample the other songs.

But not I.

If Song 7 it is, then Song 7 it is, and would be.

Nicky was saying something else but, really, I thought, who gives a fuck.

Take money, hand out ice cream.

Good ta gaow.

He hopped out of the back of the truck and said, 'Oh yeah, and watch your head coming out the back of this thing I sliced my head real bad one time,' then slammed the double doors.

I climbed into the driver's seat and buckled in.

I carefully backed up and swung the truck around as Nicky held the gate open with one hand, chain and lock in other.

If you need anything, you got my number, he said.

I pulled the truck out, hitting the fence a little.

'Sounds good,' I said.

The truck creaked and clanked.

Banged around like a motherfucker.

It was concussive.

Couldn't see shit behind me either.

I got onto a main road.

They told me not to go above fifty miles per hour but I got it to sixty right away, easy, no problem.

Everyone was checking me out.

Yeah, all right.

Who is this man hauling ass in a truck with KREEMY KROOZIN written on the side?

I looked ahead, out into the day—not just the stretch of it before me, but all of it.

The day.

The whole damn day before me.

From Clearwater down to Pinellas Park.

When I started seeing WATERFALL this and OAK GLEN that signs, I pulled off.

Slowed the truck down to a near stop.

Switched on Song 7.

Do your ears hang low / do they wobble to and fro / can you tie em in a knot / can you tie em in a bow / can you throw em over your shoulder, like a continental soldier / do your ears . . . hang . . . low . . . bing, BONG.

Barely anyone was out, though.

Just sprinklers and flags and basketball hoops.

It was late morning on a weekday—who the fuck was I gonna sell ice cream to?

I crept along, clanking in the sun, Song 7 bing-bonging.

One of the hardest parts of the job was maintaining that slow of a speed.

It felt almost painful.

Like I was doing something wrong.

Although the job was basically to drive around in a questionable-looking vehicle and attract children with candy.

This didn't occur to me until I was actually doing it: driving around a subdivision very slowly in a truck playing a song to attract children.

Up and down the blocks in a slow pattern.

'Pacmanning' was the industry term.

I drove past a woman watering her lawn.

We waved.

'Hi, howya doin,' I said.

The day began to take shape—bugs screaming, people working outside, lizards, birds, jobs, and deeds—all under this hot, blue ceiling.

Florida shit.

A young couple waved me down.

I pulled over, lowered Song 7, and got out of my seat.

Crouched over to the service window.

'Good afternoon, folks, what can I do for you?' I said, smiling.

The woman laughed. 'Oh wow, I haven't seen an ice cream man in forever.'

'Yeah, well this is my route now.'

'I'll have an ice cream sandwich,' said the man.

'Ice cream sandwich,' I said, then pointed at the woman.

'And, I'll take, a . . . nununun . . . I'll have a watermelon bomb pop,' said the woman.

I turned around, opened the cooler, and retrieved an ice cream sandwich and watermelon bomb pop.

'There you go, folks, that'll be four dollars.'

They paid and left, opening their ice cream, walking in front of the truck at a safe distance and checking for cars around the side, like pros.

I got back into the driver's seat, turned Song 7 back up, then pulled out and continued pacmanning.

I drove along with absolutely no business for another hour or so, sweating, Song 7 on repeat, drumming with my knuckles on the steering wheel.

There is something to be said for the song.

A perfect composition cycling endlessly.

You'd think it'd get annoying, but it only gets better.

I hummed and drummed to it, both feet on the floor of the truck, hoping not to kill a child.

I passed mail carriers.

I passed pairs of old women walking.

I passed shoeless drug addicts.

Construction workers.

In the back of a landscaping truck, a dirty guy on break looking at his phone, starting to bob his head as I passed.

Yes.

People waved to me.

I waved to them.

Eventually, I saw some school buses.

Kids walking around with backpacks.

Yes.

My herd.

I passed this kid—probably like three years old—and his grand-mother, who was on a motorized scooter, hunched over so much that I couldn't tell if she was awake/alive or not.

When the kid heard Song 7, he transformed.

He was taken.

I later learned this was standard.

Once the kids hear the song—once I flip the switch and go live—they go bonkers.

They go wiggy-bananas.

Something happens to their body where they seize up for a second.

They bounce in place.

They grab themselves.

They contort.

They scream.

I'm there.

I'm really there.

The ice cream man.

'Ice cream man!' yelled the kid.

He raced over to me.

He waved both hands in the air, looking at me, then back to his grandmother, who approached slowly from ten yards back, whirring along.

Waving his hands, he yelled, 'Hold on, I gotta see if my grandma has money!' and ran back to his grandma.

He was in a state of pure panic.

Which, I later found, was also common.

Is he going to leave?

Will he just drive away?

I pointed ahead a little and pulled over.

'This is my grandma, she has the money,' he said, looking up from the purse toward me again, stalling.

'Hi grandma,' I said, waving.

She waved.

He was dancing from foot to foot, gripping his backpack straps with both hands and making an exhilarated face.

'What can I get for you, sir?' I said, squinting against the sun as the kid looked at the menu, curling and smashing his dollar bills. 'Take your time.'

Song 7 binged and bonged along.

Florida shit.

'I like sour!' yelled the kid, holding up some money with his one hand, as if he were about to knight me.

'All right, how about this one,' I said pointing. 'Sour blue raspberry.'

'Yeah!' he yelled.

'Two dollars please,' I said, holding up two fingers.

He held out the money.

I had to lean far out of the service window because of how small he was.

'Only need two of these,' I said, handing him back a dollar.

I got the Popsicle out of the cooler.

The fumes felt holy on my face and neck.

I gave my client the goods and he thanked me, doing a jump with complete spin.

I returned to the sweaty driver's seat and cranked the gearshift into drive, turning up Song 7 and crawling on.

. . . do they wobble to and fro . . .

The kid kept pace for a little bit, skipping, grandma trailing behind.

He held up the Popsicle and yelled, 'This isn't too sour for me, it just tastes like blue!'

'All right!' I said, giving him a thumbs-up.

He kicked the air and licked his Popsicle.

I creaked on, turning.

Made a few more sales to elementary school–aged kids.

'Thank you ice cream maaaaaan!' yelled two girls on scooters as they pushed away.

You're welcome.

I got into the driver's seat to pull away, but two more people were approaching.

This toddler in a T-shirt and diaper came walking up with a woman probably in her twenties, urging him to walk faster.

'Sorry, thank you,' she said, smiling.

When they got to the service window, I noticed the kid was holding a bunch of plastic animal figurines.

'Got your animals,' I said.

The woman laughed and said, 'He thought when I said we had to go, that we were leaving-leaving.'

The kid eyed me, staying close to the woman's leg.

'Gotta have your things in order,' I said.

'Never know what's gonna happen,' said the woman, shrugging, putting some hair behind her ear. 'All right, baby. Come on now, pick something out.'

He walked a little closer to the menu—guided by her gentle pushing—all the while eyeing me.

I appreciated his slow-won trust.

This fella, he wasn't gonna buy ice cream from just anyone.

He picked out a sno-cone-type thing with a gumball at the bottom.

'That's got gum in it. Is that cool, Mom?' I said.

'Yeah, he loves gum.'

'Right away then,' I said.

The kid smiled a little, and when I handed him the ice cream, they walked off, waving.

It was an odd feeling, I thought, cranking into gear and turning Song 7 up.

It was maybe the first job I'd ever had where people were happy to see me.

An odd feeling indeed, to wield this kind of power.

To be this kind of force.

As near to magical as any mortal should stride.

A technician of unspeakable joy.

Braving the neon mountains to return with blue raspberry concentrate.

Tearing out sundae cone fangs from the mouths of snow beasts.

And so on.

I pacmanned forth, Song 7 at an early-evening-appropriate volume, clanking and creaking.

It was right before sunset, and temperatures were dropping just a little.

For this I was thankful.

For the truck was very hot.

The high top on the truck—meant to allow me to (almost) stand while serving ice cream—acted as a double boiler of sorts, or a pressure cooker, or some other cooking device I didn't quite understand.

All day while the ice cream stayed frozen, I slowly baked in my own sweat.

I slimed myself, stewing.

In a rolling casket of ball steam.

Like a rainforest of ball sweat.

Like I was wearing a ski mask made of sweaty ball skin.

Fuck.

I mean, fuck.

I turned down a street I hadn't been down yet.

Clanked and creaked.

There were a lot of ornamental mailboxes on either side of the street.

Dolphin: pretty cool.

Flamingo: nice.

Walrus: hell yeah.

Another bird: meh.

Shark: cool.

Florida shit.

I drove past a couple trailers.

'Ice cream man!' yelled two kids playing basketball on a bent hoop with no net.

I braked as one of them yelled inside for Mom.

But then he came back slouching, shaking his head no.

As I creaked on, his little brother ran alongside the truck.

'Take me with youuuuuuuu!' he yelled.

I drove around for a little while longer, selling maybe ten dollars' worth of ice cream, then closed out my shift idling at a cemetery with Song 7 playing low, watching the last of the sunset and eating an ice cream cone.

Can you tie them in a knot, can you tie them in a bow?

*

When I returned to the office, I opened up the back of the truck to let out the dick smell and dumped out the water and ice from the drinks cooler.

It was dark and the cicadas murmured loudly.

Sweat held my shirt against me.

All I ever wanted was a paycheck, I thought, then laughed, tossing the drinks cooler back into the truck and slamming the double doors.

I plugged the truck into the generator and went inside with the bank.

The total for the day was about a hundred dollars, with fifty of that going toward gas.

They wanted the receipt.

'Okay, so not bad,' Nicky said, scratching his lower lip with all four fingers, looking ridiculously low to the ground in his computer chair.

I put my palm against the wall and leaned.

Not sure what it was, but I already disliked Nicky.

Something about him seemed bad.

He was an asshole, yes, true, but beyond that.

He was an artist of an asshole.

A master.

Someone about whom later assholes would say, 'He's the reason I got into being an asshole.'

On the wall he hung a T-shirt with Pac-Man on it, mouth open, going toward a dollar sign.

Let me put it that way.

He was rambling about something, don't worry this and that, making better routes as time goes on, whatever whatever.

Gesturing with the money and receipt in one hand.

The other boss, Jerry, puttered around checking coolers, holding a Styrofoam cup of coffee.

He patted my shoulder as he passed and said, 'And you know, this job isn't for everyone. Maybe you find out ya don't like it, who knows.'

I went back to staring at Nicky's stupid gold crucifix.

Fuck.

'Tomorrow you're gonna wanna shoot for 150, maybe even 200,' he said. 'You know, we get you a good route going, you learn the areas and such. Get some big days going for ya. Get ya up into the fours and fives.'

'All right man,' I said.

*

The next morning I got there a little early, per Nicky's request.

The trucks had a tracking thing on them so you could replay the map and route you took on the computer.

I sat there watching a slowly moving red line on a grid representation of Pinellas Park.

We went over how I'd driven.

It was really funny.

I watched my speed on the bottom of the screen fluctuate between four to seven miles per hour, a far cry from the ideal two and not at all appropriate for pacmanning.

Sheesh.

'Yeah so, you got the pacmanning thing kind of,' Nicky said, 'But yeah just, let's try and stay in that two to three miles per hour area, K?'

The red line continued to move around, roaming the grid like a harmless shark.

*

As I got out into the fray, pulling off a main road into Sunset Glen Terrace, I thought of a new strategy.

Because even just one day in, I'd realized there was a difference between doing the job and making money.

Sure, there was pacmanning or whatever, but then what?

Pacmanning and that's it?

Let me tell you about the method of the Chuckling Squirrel.

A 'good' ice cream man enters a subdivision and drives around slowly.

But a great ice cream man enters a subdivision, idles a little bit, *then* drives around slowly.

The squirrel must chuckle for all to hear, before giving chase.

For then, the chase has a taste . . .

And so chuckles the squirrel . . .

I was already covered in sweat.

I pacmanned the entirety of Sunset Glen Terrace, making roughly eight dollars, selling a sno-cone to a man cutting his lawn and ice cream sandwiches to his neighbors.

And creaked on.

Then some dark sky came in fast, bringing rain.

Florida shit.

So I pulled over at a playground and idled there, wipers on, staring out the front window at a flooding field while Song 7 played at a low, mood-appropriate volume.

Sky totally gray.

Grass even greener.

Some kids were hiding in the tube slide.

I saw them and understood them and envied them.

I sat in silence amid the dick smell.

Can you throw 'em o'er your shoulder, like a continental soldier?

When the rain let up, I drove back out into the grid.

Terraces, boulevards, lanes, and drives.

I was to know them all.

Cul-de-sacs, courts, and dead-ends as well.

It didn't take me long to learn the fruits of the cul-de-sac.

Cut off by sidewalks or passing streets, shunned by society, the cul-de-sac sought contact.

Having been neglected, the people of the cul-de-sac embrace you with love and loose change.

Yes.

They open their arms and coin jars to you.

Today when I neared one, right on cue, I got flagged down by a pack of kids.

Cul-de-sac kids.

Each aware of their place and duty, moving as a beautiful unit, like wasps.

There were about six or seven of them, two keeping pace with me, running and screaming, while the others went to get the adult.

A near-perfect effort.

'Ice cream man ice cream man,' they yelled.

'Move back to the curb okay?' I said, doing a pushing motion with one hand.

One of the kids, recognizing the tentativeness of the situation, organized a clearing of the street as I parked the truck.

I turned down Song 7 and idled by the curb in front of what appeared to be home base.

'How's everybody doing?' I said, looking out the service window, both hands palm down on the counter.

The kids were various sizes and spirits, but all staring straight at the dope dealer.

'We're having a pizza party!' a smaller kid yelled, incapable of containing it any longer.

While we waited for the adult to come out, the kid—doing some nervous hand-wringing and tiptoeing in place—confirmed that I had arrived at the scene of an impending pizza party, the mere mention of which caused a general stir.

In addition to the pizza party, or perhaps by some insane and decadent stroke of fortune, as *part* of the pizza party, there were also plans to watch a movie.

And now, ice cream.

Wow.

I was made privy to all of this but not invited.

Wow.

'Pizzaaaaa,' one fellow yelled, either overcome with emotion or trying to keep everyone pumped, I wasn't sure.

A woman came out of one of the houses, dog running alongside her as she sorted through an immense Ziploc bag of coins.

She approached, smiling. 'Get ready!' she said. 'For some change!'

I clapped my hands and said, 'I'm ready for some change!'

Kids began approaching her with hands held out, as she scrounged through the Ziploc bag, picking out quarters.

'Okay okay, hold on,' she said, looking at me and smiling. 'Did they tell you we're having a pizza party?'

'Hell yeah,' I said.

'It's gonna be SO much fun,' she said, opening her eyes wide.

She dropped a stack of coins into a kid's hand and the kid ran up to me and dropped the coins onto my serving shelf.

'Sundae cup please,' she said, breathless.

'I'm sorry, all I have is broccoli.'

'NOOOOOOO,' said the kid, leaning her head back, smiling.

The mom laughed, dropping more coins into desperate hands.

I handed out cotton candy bars, face bars (a face bar is basically a flavored billboard of whatever cartoon), sno-cones, ice cream sandwiches, and the mom bought herself a caramel nut bar, using a giant handful of smaller coins.

The kids began to run away, all agreeing on a plan to save the ice cream for after pizza.

Pizza, THEN ice cream, THEN a movie.

Yeah!

'Have a good pizza party,' I yelled, getting back into the driver's seat and buckling up.

'Bye, ice cream man,' some of them yelled.

A van had just pulled up in home base driveway and a young man holding an impressive stack of pizza boxes exited the passenger side.

Their new god.

And I, nothing now.

Forgotten.

Used.

Useless.

Though, having reached out my hand into this sun-sprayed day, to connect with yours, outstretched—having held the ice cream together—we were joined in this ceremony forever.

I turned around in the cul-de-sac at two miles per hour, Song 7 up loud—because fuck it, the day was young.

Live young along with it, I thought.

I drove on, squinting and cooking in my own ball sweat.

*

After the first week, it all started to feel normal and I even worried less about running over kids.

I just kind of cruised around barely making money.

Hadn't been keeping track exactly but I had to be close to getting paid, I figured.

Had to be.

As I pulled into my first subdivision of the day, I quietly and tone-lessly said, 'Get some, motherfucker,' and flipped on Song 7.

Here I am.

I'm here.

But the subdivision looked empty.

Yes, I'd learned all the marks of my clientele.

Small plastic kitchens or playgrounds.

Bikes.

Miniature basketball hoops.

But there was none of that.

So I went down a kind of hidden road, off a dead-end, where the houses were just double-wides on cinder blocks.

Piles of broken shit in the front yard and lawn ornaments all over.

Plywood add-ons.

Mostly mud lawns.

Big drainage ditches.

Rusted cars surrounded by weeds.

Florida shit.

A couple kids began running alongside the truck.

'Ice cream!' they yelled.

I pulled over in front of a trailer with some people on lawn chairs out front, drinking.

A drunk guy with HARMONY tattooed on his neck came up. 'Awright Kaley, pick out whatchoo want, and get eybody else sum'n too.'

The little girl picked out stuff for everyone.

The guy said, 'Shit man, I ain't seen a ice cream man since I's a keed.'

'I'm back,' I said.

'Awright, good to hear,' he said. 'And, uh, I'll take one of those caramel nut boors, cousin.'

A mosquito landed on his forehead.

He set his money hand and his beer can hand on the serving shelf, tapping along to Song 7.

I reached into the cooler of holy fumes and gave him his ice cream.

Joined in this ceremony forever.

'You come around I'll keep you in bih'ness,' he said, biting the wrapper and pulling it open with one hand while he defended his legs from a wiffle-ball-bat-wielding youngster with the other. 'Quiddit Randy, o'I'ma beatcher ass AND eatcher ice cream, BOAH.'

Randy ran away laughing, dropping the wiffle ball bat into the grass.

I said thanks to everyone still gathered, including the obligatory 'shit out of luck' neighbor kids.

I got back into the driver's seat, instructing everyone to move across the street and out of the way.

The Ice Cream Man on his way, creaking and clanking.

. . . do they wobble to and fro?

Into the glow of midday.

I waved to some people walking their dog.

Sold a couple things to some guys working on a house.

Sold Italian ice to some kids skateboarding.

Other than that, nothing.

So the Chuckling Squirrel had to become . . . the Hunting Cheetah.

I turned down a boulevard.

Saw a guy out on his front lawn on the other side of the street.

His dogs, a giant poodle and a small orange dog, were running around and playing with each other.

The man looked like he was in his fifties, in khaki cargo shorts, sandals, a short-sleeved button-up shirt, carefully trimmed beard, and modern-looking eyeglasses.

In other words, someone who buys ice cream for himself.

'What are we doing, we want treats here?' I said to myself, U-turning on a throughway between boulevards.

He seemed to be looking so I drove past him slowly.

I waved, smiling.

He waved back and said, 'Yeah hi, get out before I call the cahhh-hahhps!' in a singsong tone.

The fuck . . .

I braked.

'What?' I said.

'I said get out. You're soliciting. Get out before I call the cops. I'm sick of it.'

Stopped in the middle of the street, Song 7 blasting, I weakly recited the boss's thing about solicitation only being door to door.

But you really can't convince someone already stupid enough to want to call the cops on the ice cream man.

You just can't.

Laughing, I said, 'Call the cops on the ice cream man?'

'That's right,' he said, nodding with his eyes open wide.

And I wondered who this man was.

This man, he does crossword puzzles.

This man, he has had problems with the neighbors over property boundaries.

He is divorced and has a son and a daughter, who visit him twice a year and politely listen to all his favorite quotes from articles about current television shows.

This man has standards for everyone but himself.

He owns collectibles.

He is an asshole.

For this person, there is no pain, and yet there is only suffering.

'Byyyee,' he said, waving at me in my rearview, as his dogs ran in playful circles around him.

I drove two miles per hour to the end of the boulevard and started back toward the guy's house.

Call the cops on the ice cream man.

What the fuck . . .

I parked nearby, like half a block away.

I saw the man talking to some concerned neighbors.

He was pointing at me and saying something, gesturing, shrugging.

I turned up Song 7.

It didn't have to be this way . . .

We didn't have to be enemies . . .

But now it's like this . . .

I geared into drive, took my foot off the pedal, and let it roll.

I saw him gesturing toward me as I moved closer and closer.

The neighbors walked away.

Song 7 in full blast, crescendoing.

DO YOUR EARS, HANG, LOW . . . bing . . . BONG.

Here I come, motherfucker.

You wanted me to leave, well now you got me.

Nearing, I slowed down even more.

The guy had his phone to his ear, and said, 'Okay, I'm calling the cops.'

'Why are you calling the cops?' I said, arm outside of the truck, shrugging and smiling.

'Because you're soliciting and obstructing traffic.'

Sissniffitiss sniff-snerz.

'I'm done with this,' he said, shrugging, 'I've had the police out here before.'

'Hey,' I said, turning down Song 7 and leaning out the window. 'FUCK you, pussy.'

I creaked away, Song 7 at full blast again, maintaining unblinking eye contact.

The world: mine.

The tears: his.

Victory: forever.

*

And then it was Labor Day weekend.

My second weekend, but my first real big holiday weekend.

Pretty much THE weekend for the ice cream business.

Plus Monday would officially be two weeks, so I'd be getting paid.

The first two days of the weekend had gone by smoothly enough.

Same shit, just a little busier.

Florida shit.

And Monday seemed no different.

I'd sold probably seventy dollars' worth of ice cream before it began to die down right before evening.

There were still a couple hours left to pacman in creaking clanks.

Needed to find a 'billionaires only' pickup basketball game.

Or just a bag with money in it.

I came to a grouping of apartment buildings off the side of a main road.

I pulled in slowly.

Kids emerged, yelling, from bushes, patios, gangways, everywhere.

Large kids, very small kids, siblings, a whole crew.

'Hi ice cweam man!' one yelled—clearly the leader.

The mayor, I thought.

I motioned for them all to move back and said, 'I'm gonna park up here.'

The mayor gathered everyone on the curb, away from the truck.

I pulled over and was swarmed.

Neon tank tops, Spider-Man shorts, pigtails, braids, rollerblades.

'What's up, everybody?' I said, getting out of my seat and leaning out the service window.

They started asking about prices.

Most bowed out, disappointed.

The mayor himself stepped up and said, 'Hi, thank you foh stopping, Ice Cweam Man. Um, can I have a popsico and a sucko pweez?'

He smiled, holding out two dollars.

'There you are,' I said, handing him the goods. 'Anybody else?'

Everyone shook their heads.

There was much sadness.

I felt it too.

'Okay, bye,' I said and went to pull into gear.

'Hoad on,' said the mayor.

He approached the window of the truck and held out the popsicle and sucker.

'I wanna retoan these.'

I looked at his hands for a second.

'Nobody ehwse, um, has any money.'

'Okay,' I said, holding the stuff. 'All right man, yeah.'

I went to put the already melting Popsicle back into the cooler.

'Wait,' he said. Then asked for the money's equivalent in gum and candy, the cheapest things on the menu.

I handed him a bunch of gum and candy, some suckers too.

He handed it out among the crew.

'Thank you, ice cream man!' they yelled.

'Have a nice Layboh Day,' said the mayor, waving.

I smiled and waved.

I told them to get everyone away from the truck, which was hard because there was still a lot of lingering excitement and fanaticism.

'Guys!' yelled the mayor, 'He needs to toan awound and not smack into us!'

He put his sucker in his mouth and motioned like an airport runway employee.

They obliged.

Because he was the mayor.

And when the way was clear, I turned Song 7 back up, cranked into gear, hit the horn a few times to wild cheering, and went on.

I left the subdivision and crossed the main road and drove around aimlessly.

The sun was starting to set.

Had about two hours until I was home, including the bullshit back at the office.

But at least I was getting paid.

Money...

My long lost friend...

Hello, yes, come in, sit down, have some soup.

I drove around to the reception of friendly but mostly uninterested faces, the breeze cooling my sweat.

Past a high school, with only a couple cars in the parking lot, lights on in the cafeteria.

Past dimming front lawns, American flags barely moving, smoke scent from somewhere.

Florida shit.

A white rabbit on someone's front lawn paused, eyeing me, then ran off.

There was always a weird sadness right before sunset, when the sky was dark blue, with orange and light pink translucence along the horizon, and it seemed as if not a single person was out, or even alive.

I heard a whistle and, 'Hey... yo!'

There was a group of younger adults, in an abandoned strip mall parking lot, hanging around a car with the doors open.

I pulled into the parking lot and parked the truck in a series of awkward and unnecessary turns.

A pale overweight guy in huge basketball shorts and stretched-out white T-shirt came *shuk-shukk*ing up in his sandals, tapping his hips.

'What's up man,' he said, looking at the side of the truck and smiling. 'Nicky still work there?'

'Wuh?' I said, leaning out the service window.

'Does Nicky still work there?' he said, looking at me. 'I used to do this shit.'

'Oh,' I said. 'Yeah, Nicky's one of the bosses.'

The guy laughed and said, 'Shit. Figures. Fuckin Jerry.'

He tapped his hips and returned to looking at the menu.

'How'd you like working for them?' I said.

He closed his eyes and shrugged. 'They still got you doing like fourteen-hour days?'

'Yeah.'

'Did they explain the deposit bullshit to you?'

'Yeah.'

He nodded, scanning the menu again.

'I should be getting paid today. It's been two weeks,' I said.

'No man. You don't get paid after two weeks, you START getting paid after two weeks.'

'What?'

'Yep, and only if that "deposit,"' he said, doing air quotes, 'is paid off, which it probably isn't, because you owe them for gas too.'

'What?'

'And, let's see, you probably spent fifty dollars a day on gas right?'

'Yeah.'

'Okay so think about how much money you've collected, subtract gas money from the bullshit cut that is yours anyway and you probably made 160 dollars for two weeks. So you still owe them for the deposit. And it's not a deposit, because you don't get it back since you "don't have to rent the truck then."'

I stared back but he just smiled.

'No,' I said. 'They hold on to it for you then give it to you when you reach three hundred or after two weeks, whichever's first.'

Still smiling, he slowly closed his eyes and shook his head. 'No dude, they'll start paying you *your cut* now, because it's been two weeks. But you still owe them three hundred dollars.'

'I'm not getting paid for the last two weeks?'

'Not at all, my good man,' he said, clasping his hands and raising his eyebrows, still smiling. 'Now lemme get a turtle bar.'

'What the fuck,' I said.

I must've been staring off, because I heard, 'Yo, hey, turtle bar, please.'

And all the features of the material world returned.

I went to the cooler and opened it, staring into the lit-up frost fumes and the neon packaging.

Those fucks . . .

Stealing from the ice cream man . . .

I shut the cooler.

Fuck.

I handed the guy the ice cream.

'I'm assuming this'll be on the house,' he said, smiling and opening the package.

'Yeah,' I said.

I gave his friends some ice cream too and then sat in the driver's seat, staring forward in idle, Song 7 on low, looking at the shop window for an out-of-business hair salon.

Some Styrofoam heads on the ground.

Florida shit.

I texted Nicky, 'So today's payday, right?'

He eventually responded, 'Jerry explained the deposit to you, right? We can talk about that back at the office.'

I bit down hard and made two fists.

Motherfuckers.

The fucking motherfuckers.

My first inclination was to just go kill them.

But that seemed bad, overall, in some way, maybe.

So I sat there 'powering down' for a little bit, Song 7 repeating at a low volume.

. . . hang . . . low . . . bing-BONG . . .

Slowly, I began some humming accompaniment.

Then slapping my hands on my thighs.

Then using my feet.

Hell yeah.

Song 7.

. . . do they wobble to and fro . . .

Yes.

Song 7 is not the song of defeat, I thought.

No.

Song 7 is the song of the champion.

The warrior, returned.

The hero, having lifted low-hanging ears, which wobbled to and fro, throws them over their shoulder to continue on.

I turned Song 7 up all the way, crackling the speaker a little.

Cranked the truck into gear and drove off.

I got out onto a main road again.

After a little bit I found the apartment complex I was at earlier.

I turned in and braked to a slow creak in the parking lot.

Gradually, they reemerged—from bushes, stairwells, between parked cars.

Siblings, friends, one and all, the kids of the various buildings.

The mayor was with them, skipping along and cracking his knuckles.

He waved.

I motioned to keep everyone back so I could pull over in the same spot as before.

I pulled over, lowering Song 7.

'What's up, everybody,' I said, nodding to the mayor and leaning out the service window on my elbows.

'Hey, how come yoh back?' said the mayor.

'Hi, ice cream man!' a younger, no doubt more stoogey fellow said, waving to me and kicking some mulch around.

It was still really hot, and the air smelled like barbecue and lawnmower exhaust.

'We don't um, have any money,' said the mayor, fidgeting with his hands. 'But maybe tomowo!'

'It's all right, I got it,' I said.

His eyes got wide. 'Fwee?' he said.

'Fwee?' yelled the smaller goon, looking at the others.

'Yeah, what do you all want?'

The excitement grew and they celebrated.

I opened the cooler.

'Ice Cream Man!' they yelled.

The Machine Operator

I went to a temp agency in Tampa.

Temp agencies are big in Florida.

There's a lot of bullshit jobs that need near-constant staffing.

The kind of jobs that ask for your weight in sweat, every day.

The kind of jobs where someone says, 'Hey, you came back!' if you show up after the first weekend.

And I should've known—by how nice and accommodating the temp office worker was—that the job would be of inverse niceness and accommodation.

I was filling out paperwork in his office.

The temp agencies always had some kind of alarmingly unclear name too, like Business Arc Solutions or Syn-Tec Distribution or whatever.

It didn't even look like an office, but instead like some people suddenly became aware that someone was about to come in expecting an office.

The temp office worker said, 'Alllllright man, lemme go plug this in and we can get you started tomorrow. For the position of'—he checked the paper—'machine operator. Cool?'

'Sounds good,' I said.

And he left to process the paperwork.

I began to envision things like: the panic-free purchasing of food, the foreknowledge of a source for rent money, and the slightly more advanced concerns/problems I'd then discover.

Hot diggity . . .

I looked around the office.

There were stacks of papers on a shelf next to me, with a few sheets pinned up on a corkboard.

One was someone's resume, for a custodial job.

It had his name in a huge font at the top and then the word 'skills' in a slightly smaller font, a bullet point beneath that said, 'am a good worker.'

Under 'previous jobs' he'd put, 'custodian/janitor' and under 'duties performed' he had, 'what a janitor do.'

The temp office employee came back and said, 'Okay, got the paperwork in, you start tomorrow at three p.m., work until midnight. Bring a lot of water and something to eat. You got steel-toed boots?'

'No.'

'Hmm, shit,' he said. 'You need steel-toed boots.'

'Okay I'll get some before the shift,' I said.

He asked what my shoe size was.

'One sec,' he said, exiting the room.

Came back with a box containing steel-toed boots in my size.

There was a sticky note on the box that said, 'DeMontero Smith.'

'Okay, this guy never showed, so you're good to go! Tomorrow at three. It's in Largo, address on that card I gave you!'

I thanked him and left.

I sat in the car, idling in the parking lot as it rained, staring at the box of boots and the sticky note.

DeMontero Smith.

Never showed.

DeMontero, where have you gone?

I imagined him crawling his way down the highway toward the boots, only to arrive, tattered and bloody, to glimpse through the window me accepting his boots.

No . . . NO!

Reaching to the sky with bloody hands . . .

The boots were really nice too.

One of the nicest things anyone has given me, actually.

Made me want to leave the boots back on the doorstep of the temp office with a note on them that says, 'I can't possibly accept these.'

And never go back.

Never show up for the job.

DeMontero, get me there.

What a janitor do.

*

I drove up to Largo the next day.

It was a plant that manufactured and boxed metal pieces.

'Contractor packs.'

The plant encompassed a vast array of machines, each producing different-sized pieces of metal.

It encompassed a dizzying heat, loud clanking, and the muffled yelling of workers.

It encompassed a small office area, where he who'd lasted longest reigned as air-conditioned overseer.

Who—when I introduced myself—had no idea who I was, and told me to go to Machine 18.

Ah yes, Machine 18.

'Go to Machine 18,' said the supervisor, bad root beer breath in my face.

I put on safety glasses, earplugs, and gloves, and walked across the floor.

Workers looked at me, in between catching metal pieces clanking out of the machines.

I saw someone welding.

Someone pushing a wheelbarrow.

People fixing machines.

People measuring parts.

Guy on a forklift.

All to a soundtrack of clanking and droning.

It was hot as fuck and smelled like gas.

I went to Machine 18.

There was a guy already working it.

He introduced himself as D'Amato, but said people call him Mato.

'What's up, Mato?' I said, slapping his hand.

'Wha's happenin, padna?' he said, smiling.

He was missing both front teeth.

Wearing a black baseball hat, an oversized black T-shirt stained with yellow paint, and wide-legged black jeans.

He turned his hat backward and explained the machine to me.

'This shit be easy,' he said, waving downward at the machine.

He started the machine by pressing two buttons at the same time, then throwing a switch.

We stood there catching parts as they came out of the machine.

Chung—down goes the top part of the machine, pressing the die onto the length of metal.

Fwoosh—die returning upward.

Skingskingsking—the metal piece coming down the chute toward us.

I caught it and jammed it up against the previous piece—*clank*.

Then the next one.

Chung . . . fwoosh . . . skingskingsking . . . clank.

Until I had twenty-five.

Then I set the stack in a box.

'See? You got it bruh.'

Four stacks to a box.

Put the box through a machine that taped it on both sides and slid it down a conveyor belt to a wooden pallet.

Stack the boxes on the pallet until there's fifty, then someone takes the pallet on a forklift.

Spray the machine down with lube.

And start over.

Like nothing had happened.

A never-ending process.

What a janitor do.

'See, this shit be easy,' Mato said, shrugging.

He told me it was only his second day.

He'd worked here five years ago, though.

'I work at this bitch years ago, padna, heh heh. Didn't realize that shit until I show up yessaday. And I'm like fuuuuuuck. See because I got fired in this bitch five years ago, heh heh.' He leaned forward with his eyebrows up and hit my shoulder with the back of his hand.

The machine die came down and sent a metal piece *skinging* down the chute.

'What?' I said, smiling.

I caught the metal piece and slapped it against the others, waiting for the next one.

'Yeah bruh, I got fired for fighting someone,' he said, pointing maybe twenty feet away.

'Right there?'

He was smiling again and laughing like *heh heh*.

He'd gotten into a fight with a boss.

A fistfight.

So they fired him.

'I pull up with o'girl today,' he said, 'and I say, "Don't go pullin away jess yet," heh heh . . . "I mighta bout to come right back."'

A metal piece came down the chute.

Sking sking sking.

Mato caught it and slammed it against the stack corralled in his other hand.

'But yeah uh,' he said, scratching his face a little, 'when I ax about him they said he died or some shit.'

He shrugged.

We laughed.

'Nice,' I said, taking over as he slammed down a stack into the box.

The machine kept working.

I hated it for its soulless determination.

I hated it for its strength.

Sometimes I watched the giant spool of metal behind the machine, seemingly undiminished no matter how long we stood there.

It weighed over three tons, Mato told me.

One had recently fallen on an employee and killed him while they were unloading it.

'Had a six-month-old kid too,' said Mato, shaking his head. 'Fork-lift du told me.'

He turned his hat to sideways.

He caught the pieces, stacked them together, and placed them in a box.

'This shit be easy, though, man,' he said, waving down at the machine.

I sprayed the machine down with lube.

I was sweating and really hungry.

My hands hurt, even with the gloves.

Pinched, cut, and dinged.

Zinged by the skinging clinkers.

'Tellin you, this shit be easy,' Mato said, slamming a stack of metal parts down into a box. 'Muffuckers don't never work no more than one day here, but this shit be easy. The machine do most the work. I'm movin back to Georgia anyhow, bruh. Fuck this shit. Give a fuck if they DO fire me again heh heh.'

Chung . . . fwoosh . . . skingskingsking . . . clank.

We caught more and more pieces.

Filled more and more boxes.

Mato kept changing the direction of his hat.

We talked about boxing.

He was excited that I knew about the boxers of his youth.

But mostly we remained quiet, in the same strange communion of people focused on the same task.

Doing what you had to do.

Every once in a while, a 'quality control tech' would wheel his cart over and ask for a piece, to test its specs.

We'd stop the machine and hand him the most recent piece to measure.

Eventually I began saying, 'My finest piece,' and slightly bowing when handing him the sample.

He seemed to enjoy it.

Mato did too.

But not as much as I did.

DeMontero, teach us laughter.

'Tangs guyce,' said the quality control tech, wheeling his cart away.

The alarm went, *boop boop boop boop* to signal one minute until break.

'Bout time in this bitch,' said Mato, turning his hat forward.

Everyone marched toward the front of the building, for cigarettes, food, phone calls, stares, and head hangs.

The alarm went, *ONG . . . ONG . . . ONG* to signal that break had begun.

Fifteen minutes, beginning after the last *ONG*.

I sat at a picnic bench alone, staring through the fence and across the street at an empty high school parking lot.

A giant American flag flew above it.

Empty football field, lit up.

Everyone congregated around the drainage ditch twenty yards away, smoking.

'Yo man, here,' said this guy, on his way to smoke, noticing I wasn't eating.

He placed two dollars on the picnic table, preemptively blocking my protest with his hand.

'Oh, I'm good, man, thanks,' I said, going to hand them back.

'Nah, I can't,' he said, still holding up his hand. 'Getchoo a pop and a candy bar.'

Then he took out a pack of cigarettes and gave me a cigarette.

I bought a candy bar and a pop.

He was right.

It was great.

DeMontero, remind us to be kind.

I had a cigarette, sitting on either side of a drainage ditch.

Someone who seemed like he'd been there a long time was complaining about the day shift.

The fuckers from the day . . .

Those day fuckers . . .

How they leave shit all fucked up.

Boxes everywhere.

Unfinished pallets.

Everything a mess.

'Every night, fuckin mess,' said the guy.

Which, I guessed, was because that's how it was left to them by the night fuckers.

Us.

Fuckers as well.

Fuckers everywhere.

Fuckers against fuckers, for the prize of biggest complainer.

Pitted against each other to hide larger power structures.

Was I sent here to bridge the gap?

Promote understanding?

What a janitor do?

No, I was just another piece.

'I swear they got shit for brains,' the guy said, of the day fuckers.

He had his safety glasses around the back of his neck.

He shook his head as he pinched off the cherry of his cigarette, putting what remained in his front shirt pocket.

I saw in his eyes that, yes, he really did hate the day fuckers.

He really did.

Which reminded me that there will always be animosity like this.

An excuse for who you are, because of who they are.

Ranging from very abstract to insanely specific.

From parts of the globe, to parts of the same country, city, street, home, flag, banner, or blood.

'I hate the day fuckers,' I said, shaking my head.

It was loud enough for a couple people close by to hear and laugh.

The alarm went, *boop . . . boop . . . boop,* signaling we had one minute.

Everyone stood up—groaning, pocketing phones, extinguishing cigarettes.

We walked back to our various machines.

The alarm went *ONG ONG ONG.*

And the machines made noise again.

*

When I got home that night, I lay in bed naked, stretching and groaning.

My feet steamed.

They were covered in blisters.

Each one throbbed according to its own spirit.

And I named them.

Justin was a well-meaning, overall nice fellow, just looking to exist.

He'd realized his situation, accepted it, and decided to move forward in a way most equal and benevolent to all sides involved, including fellow blisters.

He existed in a normal spot for a blister, was a normal size, caused normal pain, and would—no doubt—live a normal lifespan.

I didn't mind Justin.

Then there was . . . well, there were many others, even one, having taken the better part of one of my toes, of whom I dare not speak—whom I referred to simply as 'el hombre.'

A part I would not get back.

No.

For it was now el hombre's.

DeMontero, defeat no enemy for me, but lead them to me in good health.

*

'Skrippers in Atlenna be puttin blades in they weave,' said Mato, razoring open a box.

It was the end of my first week.

We were in a different area of the factory, by a garage door, sorting through damaged boxes of metal parts with a couple other guys.

Returns.

Half of the machines weren't working and there were always return boxes to sort through and salvage.

'You heard me bruh?' said Mato, scratching his elbow.

This other guy said, 'Huh? I luh Atlenna bitches.' He lightly struck his open hand with a fist. 'They bad as hell.'

'Nah I'm saying,' Mato said. 'You heard me bruh? They put blades in they weave.'

'Wuh? Thass cold! Bitches in New Yock ain on that level.'

I lifted one foot out of an untied boot and let it throb for a second.

Shit.

Felt like howling was the only correct response.

Mato stopped working and turned his hat from forward to sideways just a little. 'When they figh'in, first thing they grab's the weave, bruh. And there go a bitch, getting they hand all sliced up, heh heh.'

Everyone laughed.

'Hell yeah,' I said, pulling a wet stack of rusted metal parts out of a smashed box.

Seemed like a great move.

Putting razors somewhere you know someone else is going to grab.

Like a reverse scorpion.

Let the fools come to the stinger.

I must be more like the reverse scorpion, I thought, while becoming less and less enthused about sorting and boxing metal pieces.

It had seemed so exciting at first, so new, so wonderful.

But then it really didn't add up to much.

Mato slapped my shoulder with the back of his hand and said, 'There go a bitch getting all sliced up.'

I smiled.

Yes.

Water dripped onto me as I removed another stack of metal pieces from a damaged box.

Mato grabbed a broom and pushed some dead leaves toward other dead leaves.

'They bad as hell,' said the other guy. 'I fuck with Atlenna bitches.'

'Ay bruh, you ever fuck a German bitch?' Mato said, leaning with the broom and checking his phone. 'I'm finna go to Germany, bruh. That road where you drive however fast you want.'

Someone said, 'The autobahn.'

'Yeah, the valabahn.'

'Autobahn.'

'Bruh I'm finna be up on that bitch going hunnit-eighty in a Lambo. You ever fuck a German bitch? Ey, you heard me, bruh?'

'Nah,' said the other guy, looking at his phone and holding a half-folded box.

'Man,' said Mato, 'You ever fuck a Russian bitch?'

'Nah man, I ain'ever fucked no Russian bitch.'

'Man I KNOW they ain't be likin our kind, I hollat dis Russian bitch, you heard me, and she look at me like she'a up and kill my ass.'

Everyone laughed.

Mato did a pose and made a face and said, 'She said she'a up and kill my ass,' then walked roughly twenty feet away in a comical fashion, pumping his arms and legs.

People were laughing really hard.

'Mato you stupid,' someone said.

Mato came back up and muttered, 'She'a up and kill my ass.'

He razored open another box.

We sorted some more.

It sucked.

Counting to make sure each smashed box had the right quantity, then reboxing them.

Bullshit dripping all over.

Sharp metal parts.

Floppy cardboard boxes.

What's worth saving and what's not.

NOTHING!

Mato and company carried on an impressively nuanced and thoughtful examination of some contemporary musical artists' personal lives—on matters of finance, romance, and general existence.

They were informed, decisive, and not at all forgiving.

Dead leaves blew into the work area, scraping across the ground under the opened garage door by which we worked.

Sky outside blue and orange.

Assuring me—though only for a moment—that life was best licked.

And never really finished.

No real finish line.

Just a single point from which all other extensions are available.

What a janitor do.

DeMontero, can you hear me?

*

Each day began to feel faster.

Or maybe just further away.

Each day meant less and less.

I lost a bunch of weight as well as the feeling in some toes.

Standing in front of a machine for nine hours, catching metal parts and stacking them in boxes.

Long pieces, medium-sized pieces, oddly shaped pieces, and, worst of all, the small square-shaped pieces.

Oh those little squares . . .

Fasteners, they were called.

Every piece had the potential to hurt you in some mild to severe way, but none like the fastener.

Skipping down the chute—small, resolute, and strong.

Like a blunt throwing star.

I was working the fastener machine today, swearing and grinding my teeth.

Even with the gloves on, they could still catch you the right way.

Corner dinging right off your knuckle.

Dinging off the bone in a way that caused some kind of deeply cold feeling.

Like your entire skeleton coughed.

A zinging.

Zingers and bone shakers.

It reminded me that every job, even ones almost entirely unlikable, had an element that was the worst.

The opposite of a cherry on top.

And for me, it was the fasteners.

I pressed both activate buttons on the fastener machine and flipped the switch and the die went down hard, CHUNG.

A fastener flew down the chute and zinged off my knuckle and my finger went numb for a second.

I quietly said, 'You motherfucking piece of shit,' through gritted teeth, my eyes bulging.

I'd been there long enough to become less concerned about hiding my anger.

The murderous thoughts in general, involving metal pieces.

How I wanted to bring one down on someone's head like an axe.

Or drag one across my stomach and free my guts.

Fucking fasteners.

But then the machine stopped working.

Shoooong.

It moved no more.

Its ghost already floating away.

Yes . . .

Fuck yeah . . .

Praise be!

I smiled.

'Go work on 13 with Jaime,' yelled the foreman, bad root beer breath into my face, after catching me not working for ten seconds.

One of his jobs was to walk around and spy on the workers.

If you stopped working for more than fifteen seconds, he popped out from behind somewhere and asked you what you were doing.

I didn't dislike him, though, because on one of my first shifts, I sat in the break room and watched him stare straight forward at the wall while eating pizza out of a Ziploc bag and chugging root beer.

Sometimes he still had pizza in his mouth while chugging the root beer.

And I knew then that, for whatever reason, I could never dislike him.

He'd always be something to me.

I went to Machine 13.

There was an older man working it.

We shook hands.

'Hey,' I said.

He kind of explained what I had to do.

Couldn't really speak English and I couldn't really speak Spanish, but there was enough overlap to understand.

These long metal pieces were going to come down the chute and, yep, you guessed it, we had to catch and stack and box them.

All right, sure.

I mean why not, I'll be here.

He started the machine.

Chung.

Skingskingsking.

These pieces were new to me.

I had not done them.

They were arm's length and had a corner on each end, like a giant bottle opener.

Like fucking swords.

I caught the first couple and stacked them half-assedly.

Getting them to fit together seemed like a cruel puzzle.

The guy tried showing me how to stack them, smiling the whole time in a way that suggested he was reading my mind, which was thinking, 'Yeah, fuck this shit.'

So, whatever.

We caught the skinging clinkers as they came down the chute.

Winding down the three-ton spool of metal.

Going pretty well until one of the metal pieces *sking*ed the wrong way, took a hop, and went across my bicep.

Split my meat real good.

Took a second to bleed but then oh yeah, it bled.

The guy said something.

I stared at him as he mouthed things I couldn't hear.

Blood ran down my arm.

I did a thumbs-up and motioned for us to keep working.

But he stopped the machine, staring at the blood from behind his crooked safety glasses.

Shoooong.

'It hurt you?' he said.

'I'm good,' I said, wiping some of the blood with my T-shirt.

But it was bleeding decent then.

He tried to explain something involving his arms.

Looked like the motion of putting on lotion.

'You gonna . . . ah, dey have de . . . ah . . .' he said, looking around.

Eventually he just motioned for me to follow him, motioning over his shoulder.

We walked through the factory.

We passed this other worker, who saw my bloody arm and threw both hands down like he'd just lost in poker and said, 'Aw man. Now they gone have to put that shit on the calendar.'

He was referring to our injury chart, where—if we remained without incident for a month—we got free lunch.

I laughed and said, 'Just don't tell anybody.'

He gave me an angry look and walked away.

We walked over to a small supply area where they kept gloves and earplugs and vests and shit.

He handed me two arm sleeves made of some kind of strong, interlocking fiber.

Like powerful socks for my arms.

I cleaned my bloody arm off in the drinking fountain, covered the wound with a wad of paper towel, and put the arm sleeves over my arms.

The arm sleeves—they were very powerful.

Yes, they strengthened me.

Quite frankly, I felt invincible with them on.

I could see why the guy working the machine already had them on.

DeMontero, keep me safe.

I strutted back out into the workplace looking for the nearest skinging clinker I could find.

Where you at, lil clinkers?

I returned to the machine.

Chung.

Skingskingsking.

The clanging skingers.

I caught them and stacked them.

No problem.

Stacked the fuck out of them actually.

Boxed the fuck out of them too.

I finished off a pallet.

No fucking problem.

DeMontero, protect me.

'Good?' said the other guy with his thumb up.

'Yeah man, thank you,' I said, smiling in what seemed like an insane way, my thumb up as well.

We worked for a couple more hours.

Sweating.

My back moaned.

It seemed, I thought, more or less, time for the workers to gather in the middle of the factory to begin fighting in front of rich people for money.

Something.

Anything.

But instead, just more metal pieces.

Chung . . . fwoosh . . . skingskingsking . . . clank.

Contractor packs.

Metal pieces.

Sometimes I wondered about all the great decks/houses/projects that would come from the metal pieces.

The towns, cities, backyards, schools, playgrounds, and whatever elses these parts would build.

But mostly I didn't.

Reverting to that age-old—nearly invincible—philosophical question of, 'Who the fuck gives a shit?'

What a janitor do.

DeMontero, get me there.

*

On break, I had a cigarette with everyone.

We sat around the drainage ditch.

Mato sat on the sheet metal drainage pipe, positioning himself on the pipe with a leg on either side.

'Notice I ain be puttin my shit in front of this bitch,' he said. 'You ain never know the fuck gone come outta that bitch. We in Florida.'

People laughed.

Mato said, 'You ain *never* know the fuck gone be comin out this shit, I'm talmbout.' He stood up and walked away in a comical fashion, pumping his elbows and knees as he walked.

People laughed.

This was the key to Mato's material.

Walking away in a comical fashion after repeating what he'd just said.

Someone said, 'Shit, Mato. You stupid.'

'You heard me?' Mato said, walking back to the group, laughing. He sat back down on the pipe, legs on either side. 'You ain never know the fuck comin out this bitch.'

One guy gestured to his friend and said, 'This guy from Cuba, he don't give a fuck, he eat that shit. We got fish with legs in Cuba.'

The guy next to him laughed and said something in Spanish.

People laughed.

'Where you from, homey?' Mato said. 'You Messican?'

'Nah, he's from Cuba, man, I just said that. We all are.'

Mato asked about Cuba.

What was it like there.

Should he go there.

Castro had just died.

Someone said that all the things you owned aren't really yours there, and you're not really free.

Mato said, 'Whatchoo mean? Like my TV? I ain own that bitch? That bitch ain't mine?!'

'Hell no, bro,' said a younger guy, doing something on his phone. 'That bitch is not yours, bro. And there ain't shit you can do about it.'

Another said, 'He worry bout TV . . .'

Everyone laughed.

'Hell no, I fight them bitches,' said Mato.

'They'll just put you in jail or shoot you. They don't give a fuck there, bro. What are you talking about.'

Someone said something in Spanish and a bunch of people laughed.

'Man, how you goan shoot a brotha?' said Mato. 'They'ont be likin the brothas down in Cuba? Heh heh.'

'Nah man, they don't give a fuck about you there. Prison here is like a fucking resort compared to Cuba bro. You end up in prison in Cuba, you're fucked worse than death, bro.'

A bunch of people laughed.

'Feed you water and shoogar,' said another guy. 'Beat you ass every fucking day until you die.'

Someone said something in Spanish again, and everyone laughed.

Mato did his own nonsense Spanish, which he did anytime too many people were speaking Spanish around him.

'Bassa la cassa de la pasta, PUTA!' he said.

Some people laughed.

'Mato, you should move to Cuba, man, you'd love it,' someone said.

'What about my house?' said Mato. 'That nigga own that shit too?'

'Yup,' someone said.

'What?' Mato said. He stood up again, cigarette in mouth while holding up both fists in the classic fisticuffs pose. 'Man, fuck that. I be figh'in a bitch. Wussuh, Caysh-dro. I whoop yo ass, bitch, heh heh.'

He lowered his head laughing, still holding up his fists.

I was laughing.

The Cubans were laughing.

Anything that would've come out of that drainage pipe would've been laughing.

'I whup yo comniss ass, muthafucka, talkin bout hassa la bassa de pasta. Gimme my rights!'

He was doing insane punches and keeping his head leaned back, closing his eye to the smoke of the cigarette.

'Bro,' said a Cuban. 'You ain't shit there. They'd just shoot you. Why the fuck would anyone care about your rights? Seriously man, I want you to tell me why anyone would give a fuck.'

The Cubans were laughing.

'Whatchoo mean?' said Mato.

'Bro,' one of them said.

And they explained how they were all basically slaves.

It wasn't like here.

They had no control.

And that's why they left.

Building boats in the middle of the night.

They talked about how people celebrated in Little Havana when Castro died.

One guy got real serious and talked about how the government took most of his family, for being religious, and he never saw them again.

They talked about being 'disappeared.'

Mato said, 'How they gone disappear me? I'm fat as hell.' He laughed, cigarette down to the filter. 'Ayuh, how many underage bitches you thank Fidel be fuckin? Might as well. Shit, you the boss. Who gon suck my dick tonight? Shit, get in line f'that shit. Bitches with no teeth to the front of the line heh heh! You suck my dick I give you extra veshtables or some shit,' he said, laughing harder.

It was hard not to laugh at everything he said, because he laughed at everything he said, and his laugh was hilarious.

Other people were either laughing or shaking their head or doing both.

The warning bell rang.

Boop, boop, boop.

Finishing cigarettes.

Pocketing phones.

One guy said goodbye to his daughter, who he'd videochat with every night right before she went to bed. 'Bye sweetie,' he said, doing a kiss to the screen.

A small voice said, 'Night, Daddy.'

We all got up, groaning and swearing.

I limped, trying to force the toenail on my pinky toe back into place.

My machine partner walked next to me.

He carefully said, 'Know why you don't have ah, de communism here?'

'No,' I said.

He held up both hands as if holding a gun and said, 'De ryfo.'

'The rifle,' I said, smiling.

He nodded, smiling behind crooked safety glasses.

The rifle.

What a janitor do.

DeMontero, protect us all.

The factory welcomed us back with heat.

*

Supervisor had me work the remainder of the shift on a riveter.

Sitting in a chair riveting pieces of metal together.

You grab one piece, set it on the riveter, set another piece on top so they overlap a certain way, then put the pointer finger of each hand into the sensors on either side.

Shuggunk.

Riveted.

I sat there for a couple hours, stacking metal parts, pressing buttons and fastening shit together, chucking them into boxes.

Line up the pieces.

Press the buttons.

Shuggunk.

If the riveter misses, do it again.

Throw the new piece into a box.

It seemed, overall, better than any other job there because at least you could sit.

But then that hurt too.

Toward the end of the shift, my riveter started failing, spitting out bent rivets all over.

It pissed me off way more than it should.

Because it shouldn't have pissed me off at all.

Mato was sitting next to me at a riveter, looking at his phone.

'Man, [athlete] a beast this year,' he said to a guy across the table at a different riveter.

'For real,' said the other guy.

Then they had a conversation around whether or not you should bring your woman to the beach.

There was so much ass there anyway, one posited, bringing your woman just ruined everything.

One man in particular seemed troubled by the abundance of ass at the beach.

He was so utterly confused why anyone would—given the amount of ass already at the beach—bring more ass to it, especially when that one ass prevented you from enjoying all of the others.

I had to admit that he danced with truths.

I started sweeping around my area.

I swept the bent rivets into a dustpan and dropped them into the trash.

I kept a handful of the rivets, and some other small metal pieces I found, because they looked like valuable gems or coins or something.

I'd started a collection at home.

It felt nice to have them.

I didn't ask myself why or ridicule myself for wanting the magical coins.

I just took them.

Because why not.

I tied off the trash and took it out and enjoyed the breeze and the dark night sky.

Largo, Florida.

Humid darkness and the highway whirring, not far off.

The fifteen-minute 'end of shift' warning alarm rang.

Boop boop boop.

The siren of love.

We observed fifteen minutes of mock-cleaning, as well as throwing big balled-up rolls of plastic into far-off garbage cans.

Mato hid off to the side of a machine, leaning on a control panel and staring out.

It looked like he was contemplating the beginning of time.

'I'm done, bruh,' he said to me, shaking free of his stare.

Then we all got in line for the punch clock, one minute remaining.

No one ever worked the last minute.

It was a tiny rebellion that would one day lead to all the minutes.

But you had to start with one.

Never ever ever work the last minute.

What a janitor do.

Sweating, shirts off, undershirts steaming, lunchboxes in hand, smelling awful, lube wrinkled but elated.

All looking forward to the future: a single wide door propped open and leading to the parking lot.

Nobody had anything to say anymore.

Mato was in front of me, quietly singing.

I stared at the safety rules on the corkboard, featuring the same featureless man receiving injuries of all kinds.

Electrocution.

Puncture wound.

Cuts.

Broken bone.

Mato started singing louder.

'Fuck *up*, Mato,' someone said.

Others laughed.

Mato smiled and laughed, a hoarse *heh heh*. Then he said, 'Iss all good, I'm jess playin.'

An older man, very small and hunched and skinny, stood off to the side of the line holding some scrap metal, chewing his toothless gums.

His eyeglasses made his eyes look huge.

He was the guy who worked the forklift all day.

I'd never heard him speak.

He wore a baseball hat for a towing company, blued tattoos on his forearms.

He adjusted the scrap pieces in his arms.

'Why you takin that shit, Elton?' Mato said.

Elton said, 'Fixin ta make uh pin. Got me a puppy.' He pushed his glasses up.

'Oh shit, you got a puppy, Elton?' Mato said, turning his hat from backward to backward/sideways, swaying in place as the final bell rang and the line began moving.

'Yizzir,' said Elton. 'He a bastard doe. Needa learn himself sum'n fore I killem.'

Mato laughed and said, 'Oooooh you gotta grab that sumbitch by the neck and'—he motioned with his other hand—'Wuhhhhap! Right on at ass. Thass how I'm brangin it. Whapppp, right on at ass!'

Elton said, 'I believe thass right,' and nodded, smiling a little, his huge eyes blinking.

'Whap!' yelled Mato again.

'Mato shut the fuck up!' somebody yelled.

The line had stalled.

Faulty punches.

A series of beeps.

People started yelling variations of 'hurry the fuck up' and/or general sentiments of doom wished upon the offender.

'Fuck you, Carlos, hurry *up*,' someone yelled from way back. 'Andale pinche puta.'

'Bassa de la HASSA, amigo,' yelled Mato.

Carlos punched out and smiled, saluting as he walked off.

The happiest person in the world.

None higher than he right then.

Until the next guy punched out.

Free . . .

Mato punched out, turned his hat backwards, singing loudly.

I punched out.

Yes . . .

DeMontero, get me home.

Bless you for another night.

I was sweat gelled and sore.

Walking through the parking lot.

Dark and humid.

I idled in the car with the radio on, staring forward for a few minutes before driving off.

Down the smaller roads lined with factories and gas stations, then southward on I-275, toward St. Pete.

The highway was mostly empty, just a long line of lights and glowing road.

But it felt special.

Something only for me.

When I got home, I parked, and sat in the car.

Noticed I'd had a staticky radio station on the whole time.

But then it focused and came in clearer, playing opera.

So I sat and listened.

On a dark street.

Opera with occasional light static.

I leaned the seat back and listened for a while.

Hands throbbing from the zinging clinks.

Shoulders filled with thorns.

Back moaning.

Feet aching as though boiled and beaten.

Haha.

I only had a couple weeks of temp work left before the company either hired me or put a cigar out on my forehead and told me to fuck myself.

But I'd already decided I was moving.

Wasn't sure where but.

Fuckem.

Catch your own zinging clinkers, you fucks.

DeMontero, heal me.

I closed my eyes and breathed in.

Trying to put a giant nothing between me and whatever else.

To stop it all for one second.

Just stop everything.

The where I was as who I was.

Then nothing.

Then the where I am as who I am, separated and begun anew.

One dropping back like a part of a train let loose.

The other moving forward.

To separate yourself and start again.

But just a little.

Not so long you lose yourself.

But enough.

And it worked.

Oh yes, it worked.

I turned my head and opened my eyes, looking at a palm tree swaying gently in the moonlight.

The top of the palm dark and angular.

Like a pom-pom of knives, cheering.

Cheering on whatever motor runs this shit, and always will.

Chung.

The one that never stops.

Fwoosh.

The one that always runs.

Skingskingsking.

And us, its metal parts.

Clank.

Boxed up and ready to use.

Some to build great things, some broken and returned.

'What a janitor do,' I said softly, and smiled.

MICHIGAN

Geese

I was at the hardware store with my friend, Danny, a seventy-year-old Marine.

His friend, the owner, was sitting on a stool.

They discussed their ideal loads/powders for hunting different birds.

No other customers in the store.

Danny was championing a certain shotgun load he used for geese when he broke off and said, 'Gosh it's so sad though, the way the other goose comes back. After the one gets killed, the other flies back to check on it, after everything settles. They won't leave the body. They stay right by its side.'

He'd been in gunfights, wars—riots and bar brawls as a police officer—but the geese . . .

He was quiet for a second, then clicked his teeth, nodding, and said, 'Anyhow, kinda innaresting.'

I stared out the front window, at an old lady shuffling across the street with her walker.

Reminded—as I was every once in a while—that we all go out like babies.

Dragon

My friend and I were driving down US 12, dark woods on either side.

On the way to return a tent he'd borrowed from one of his coworkers.

'I can never remember which one it is,' he said, slowing down to check the occasional, mostly unmarked, entrance.

Mouths to long driveways that went deep into the woods.

Couple of NO TRESPASSING signs.

'Think it's this one,' he said.

We turned in.

Drove slowly, until the headlights touched a shed.

'Hope we don't get shot,' he said, turning off the car.

'Ha.'

It was totally silent.

I mean nothing.

And then a light came on as a screen door opened, hundreds of bugs hovering above it.

Dogs barked.

'Wuddup guys!' yelled my friend's coworker. Then he yelled, 'Shut the fuck up!' to the dogs and waved us toward the house.

Inside, the dog pack greeted us—a medium, overweight, sausage-like dog with a gray muzzle, a smaller dog, and a dog so small I thought it was a chipmunk at first.

They barked, then wagged their tails, ears going down.

My friend and I set the tent down against the wall.

The house looked like a tornado hit it.

Or like the contractor gave up about 65 percent of the way.

Bare plywood and nails all over.

Tarps.

Aquariums filled with garbage.

A gigantic tree branch—as in, still part of a living tree—went through the middle of the house.

I sat in an office chair and my friend sat on a milk crate.

'Sorry the place is fucked. I'm barely here anymore. Heh oops.'

The overweight dog came up to me and put his greasy head in my lap—eyes red and watery, goop in the corners.

'Hey buddy,' I said, rubbing his head.

'Oh man, that's Dragon,' said the host, pulling the tent into a corner. 'Old Dragon . . . he's such a dumbass, but that's my guy.'

Dragon's eyes were closing, head heavy in my lap.

'Man, it's a miracle he can even walk. That motherfu'er was paralyzed for *four* months heh. Couldn't move at all from the neck down.'

'What?' said my friend. 'For real?'

'Yuuup. He used to *love* to kill raccoons. But one time, one a them fuggers got him good n'heh. And it had some disease or some shit. He got spinal meningitis heh. This motherfu'er couldn't move for *four* months. We had to baby him.'

'Dragon, is that true!?' I said.

But Dragon was dead to the world as I worked his jowls.

'Alls he could do was lie there all day. When he barked, his entire body shook, but he couldn't move.'

Everyone laughed.

'Innat that right, Dragon?' said his owner, as he walked toward me.

He scooped Dragon up, one arm underneath the butt/back legs, and one around the chest.

'He'd bark, and just be lying there, spasming on the floor n'heh.'

He kissed Dragon on the head.

Dragon looked reluctant about—but ultimately resigned to—being carried around.

'Dude, it was nuts. We had to carry his ass outside like this for him to shit. It was a race of getting him outside, hoping he didn't shit on your arm.'

He lowered Dragon and lifted him back up a few times.

Dragon grunted.

I was laughing.

With little clicking sounds, the very small dog approached my friend.

'Oh hey there!' said my friend, as the dog wagged its tail at his feet.

'Ohp, now you did it. That's Lady. Give her any attention and she won't leave you alone heh.'

My friend picked Lady up and put her in his lap.

She lay down immediately, wagging her tail and resting her chin on his arm.

Then she breathed out, looking off into the distance with strangely sad eyes.

Eyes that said, 'Why, mi amor?'

'Well look at that,' I said.

Everyone watched as my friend petted the tiny dog.

And it seemed strange to me.

That this thing trusted my friend.

Knowing nothing of his intentions.

In a world of cruelty.

This little helpless thing sought security in a stranger.

Like every thing was just a smaller thing looking for a bigger thing to take care of it.

Paralyzed and helpless and needing to shit, looking to be scooped up and relieved.

'Aw I hate to do this, Lady, but we gotta get going,' said my friend.

He set her down and as soon as her tiny legs touched the ground she ran up to the third dog, who'd gone to sleep.

Lady bit at the sleeping dog's ears and its eyes popped open, lips curling back.

'Awesome, thanks for coming by, fellas!' said my friend's co-worker, setting Dragon down.

Dragon huffed over to police.

We said goodbye and left.

The screen door whapped shut.

Back out into the darkness.

Sound of a distant motorcycle.

Otherwise nothing.

Bugs.

We walked back down the driveway to the car and backed out slowly.

Through the darkness.

Down the long driveway.

Sticks snapping.

'I have a feeling we're gonna crash,' said my friend, as we stopped by the main intersecting road, host to many fatalities.

'I do too.'

I'd been thinking about it the whole way there.

And for a second, right then, I felt it.

Like a peach thrown against the wall.

I looked down the road.

On one side, only a thin bit of moonlight on the curve where the road disappeared over a hill.

On the other side just darkness.

Zero visibility.

'What a way to die,' said my friend. 'Just T-boned right here.'

And we backed out into the middle of the road—stopped—and began driving again.

Spared by the bigger thing, once more, maybe.

The Stag

I live in an apartment on the outskirts of a small town.

It's by a large field of lavender, which has just begun to die.

Behind that, it's woods and wetlands, with fallen trees, small areas of marsh, signs about poison ivy, and some workout stations made of wood and metal.

I'm there now, doing pull-ups before work.

Tonight I have to work a three-hundred-person wedding.

But that's tonight.

For now, I'm free.

The sunlight is golden on the trees, leaves changing color, air beginning to cool.

I hop up and grab the pull-up bar and do ten pull-ups, hop back down.

The blood is moving through my body.

I look out across the large, bright field.

A rustling reveals a family of deer running into the clearing.

A large one and three smaller ones.

Boo!

They disappear.

They go somewhere else.

They're gone.

*

I arrive at the reception hall two hours before the guests.

My boss is straightening place settings at long wooden tables.

'Hey hey,' I say to him.

He says hi, looking very tired.

'What's goin on, lavender man?' I say, referring to his lavender-colored vest/shirt. 'Check out lavender man, everybody.'

My coworkers laugh.

My boss smiles.

I tie a black apron over my black button-up shirt and black dress pants.

All black.

The point of all black, in addition to just being uniform, is to re-move me/us as much as possible.

In the dimly lit hall, wearing all black makes me, basically, a shadow.

Designed to create the illusion that the environment is serving the guests.

That I'm not really there.

Just hands in the air.

My boots *tok tok* in the large empty hall as I look around the room.

The head table lined up in the middle of the room.

There's an antique dresser behind the table.

A rug and a couch off to the side.

'Nice, very nice,' I say.

The event planner runs around with candles and plants.

Boxes of glass things.

Gold cursive cards to mark table numbers.

Name cards.

Hanging glass orbs with electronic candles in them.

Special chandeliers.

People on ladders hanging a big banner of ivy and lights over an arch.

There?

Right there.

I help my coworkers place silverware.

Steak knife then butter knife on right, salad fork then dinner fork on left.

Order.

A process.

The silverware is spotty.

Everyone's tired.

Bartenders set up glasses, mixers, ice, wine bottles, and cases of beer.

Photographers survey the room.

The DJ sets up speakers.

We move tables just slightly.

Huge, heavy tables built by Amish people.

Chairs.

Stacking and unstacking chairs.

I look outside at a silo, around which are chairs and a small tent thing from yesterday's ceremony.

Empty chairs on green grass beneath blue sky and white cloud.

Yesterday's ceremony is today's task.

'Two families will become one tonight,' I say, in an evil voice.

My coworkers laugh.

'Who's on "Living Ottoman" duty tonight?' one says.

It's a joke we made up.

Living Ottoman.

I right water glasses and polish them, base then rim.

'No, but, I just hope everyone enjoys themselves tonight,' I say. 'That's what I'm here for.'

My boss smiles, straightening some knives. 'I can never tell if he's being serious or not.'

'I'm being serious right now, lavender man. It's our job to help aid in this union. If that's not what you're here for, you get the hell out right now.'

I continue polishing glasses.

Looking out the window.

There's a few crows.

They're waiting to fly me back to the woods.

Come with come with!

You're so beautiful, I think.

Boo!

*

In the kitchen, everyone hustles.

It's steamy.

'Wuddup Shane!' I yell, to the dishwasher. 'You doing good?! You doing fucking good?!'

The dishwasher smiles. 'Shit, you see very well I'm on top of it. Rogue agent.'

At some point he'd begun referring to us as 'rogue agents.'

And at first, I didn't understand.

But then I did.

Rogue agents.

Sometimes he'd say it while putting his back against mine, doing a two-handed 'guns up' motion.

I liked Shane.

He had gray teeth and looked anorexic.

He lived in the trailer park by my apartment complex.

Same look on his face always; only his mouth moved.

He listened to music through a portable speaker.

Some type of music I'd never heard.

Sounded like music for a video game with an eastern/dance tone.

Like, unless you were riding a horse made of shadows through a forest in Romania, on a revenge mission to kill a werewolf—holding an emerald sword, your eyes red and lightning filled—I'm not sure it was appropriate.

But that's what rogue agents do.

Live outside the rules.

Outside your petty reality.

'Rogue agents,' Shane says, nodding.

We bump elbows.

'Rogue agents,' I say.

Shane smiles.

'Bro, if they don't sort the knives tonight bro,' he says, suddenly serious, 'I'm gonna snap, man. I mean it.'

Sometimes people forgot to sort the sharp knives from the other silverware.

And Shane has been stabbed many times.

He has survived many extremely minor stabbings.

He often displays the Band-Aids on his hands to prove it.

'Shane, I'm gonna tell those motherfuckers what to do, and they're gonna do it. They will all submit. I can't have an injured rogue agent.'

He holds up both hands, fingers splayed. 'Bro I got stabbed so many times, I'm gonna snap.'

And he's serious.

He's totally serious.

'Don't snap,' I say.

'Bro, I'm gonna have ta snap. I'm serious. Fuck it though. Tomorrow's my mom's birthday,' he says, lifting up his backward hat and lowering it again.

Says he's taking her out.

'Nice, I hope you have a good time. Tell your mom happy birthday.'

He says they will have a good time, detailing a deal happening at the place they were going.

'That's a hell of a deal,' I say. 'I wish I was going with.' Then I stare off for a second. 'All right, you ready for this shit man? You ready for this?'

'I'm ready!'

More servers show up.

We stand around listening to the lead server, who has written an itinerary on a whiteboard.

Strategies for the evening.

The process.

Guests come in at.

Ceremony at.

Cocktail hour at.

Speeches at.

Dinner served at.

Dancing at.

Last call at.

Sparkler send-off at.

Guests out at.

Vendors out at.

Done.

Victory.

Sleep.

'Gonna be a long one, kids,' says the lead server. 'Pain death mur-der kill, et cetera.'

'But to aid in eternal love, what is pain?' I say.

Sandy laughs.

She's standing next to me, arms folded.

She's four feet tall, boy's haircut.

'Scrappy.'

She goes to Notre Dame.

We became friends through inappropriate joking.

Mostly about dicks, but lately about our/everyone's moms.

'You ready, Scrappy?' I say.

'Your mom's ready . . .' she says, smiling, 'for sex with me.'

We laugh.

'Nice.'

When the meeting disbands, she and I hang out in the kitchen.

She toothpicks meatballs and places them on a fancy tray.

I funnel salad dressing into glass containers.

Somebody has stolen my trusty blue cheese dressing funnel.

'Why they gotta do that shit, Shane?' I say, throwing around utensils and contraptions on the shelf. 'You can do a lot to a man, but taking his blue cheese funnel, that's too far!' I yell, 'That's too far!' at an incredible volume.

I accuse people coming in and out of the kitchen of stealing my blue cheese funnel.

Every excuse they give I label 'convenient.'

'Ceremony's about to start,' says the lead server coming back into the kitchen, finger over his lips and looking at a piece of paper.

Everything is pretty much on hold until that's over.

The legal end.

The business end.

Da paperwork.

The shortest, least interesting portion of the whole thing.

My coworkers and I have begun using the classic 'fingers rotating over each other' hand signal during this part.

Music plays from the hall.

A blessing.

A speech from the priest.

A reading from the parents.

Some words from bride and groom.

The couple is married.

Cheering.

Acoustic guitar music.

Official.

People clapping, stomping their feet as the bridesmaids exit arm in arm with the groomsmen.

Then the bride and the groom.

Two teams become one.

Something has happened.

But really it's nothing.

All just some play.

Some audition.

Everything anyone ever does, or expects done by another, is part of some audition.

You're always auditioning.

Every move, every choice, every look, every word, enters the audition.

The people getting married, they're auditioning for their parents and relatives, after auditioning for each other.

How the food was.

How the bride looked.

A description by one attendee to a neighbor the next time they cross paths.

Even me.

The way my hair looks to the guests in the reception hall, the words I use, my voice, the way I walk, everything I do.

All taken into account on someone's ledger.

The audition.

You can opt out of the audition, but not really.

You're still performing, just careless of score.

Which adds up.

Until, eventually, you're just holding the lights for someone else's audition.

And what then?

'Quit whackin it,' Sandy says. 'It's go time.'

'Whack(in) it' is a phrase Sandy used to mean virtually anything.

'All right let's go,' says the lead server. 'Everybody go.'

We go out and move the room around behind a closed curtain while the guests go to the bar for cocktail hour.

We stack and unstack chairs.

Move tables.

Check the map and make adjustments.

The room is ready for dinner.

After that, I bus glasses in the bar/cocktail area while Sandy and others distribute appetizers.

Navigating through the undrunk small talk.

The hugs.

Cologne and makeup.

Babies fawned upon, passed around.

Men hold up hands for little kids to punch.

Little girls twirl in dresses, holding chocolate-covered pretzel rods, the chocolate of which is the only part eaten.

Things are said.

Family news reviewed.

Who's going to what school.

Who's doing what.

Who's who.

I grab some glasses, wink at a server carrying a tray of appetizers.

Meatballs.

Pretzel bites.

Crab cakes in tiny bamboo boats.

How do I eat this.

Can I eat the little tray thing.

A glass breaks.

I go to the kitchen and grab the broom and dustpan.

Sandy is reloading her wooden tray.

'Are they enjoying the balled meat, Scrappy?' I say.

She says, 'They have been putting their lips all over my balls of meat.'

The head cook, Annie, yells, 'Knife!' and comes around the corner holding a knife. She says, 'Pfft when was the last time you handled some balls, girl.'

Sandy says, 'I haven't handled balls in a long long time, thank God.'

She walks through the door holding her wooden tray.

'How you doing, Annie?' I say.

Annie smiles at me with her eyes closed and says, 'Hey honey.'

She's extremely short with a butch haircut, glasses that make her eyes look huge, and a pentagram necklace.

There are burns and other scars all over her arms from the kitchen.

She points to a kitchen worker who is looking at her phone.

Annie holds up the knife and mouths, 'I'm gonna kill her.'

'Always with the killing stuff,' I say, shaking my head.

The first shift I worked there, she told me she was getting ready to kill her ex-husband.

I told her I'd help her dispose of the body.

That's how we became friends.

That's how we remain friends.

She proposes violence and I offer to help.

That's all some of us need sometimes, to know someone else is in on some violence.

Just nice to know you'd be helped.

The last couple weeks Annie has been wearing Halloween-themed T-shirts/blouses, with, like, a smiling pumpkin on the front and SPOOKED OUT! (eyes in the *oo*) beneath it.

Sometimes a witch hat.

Pajama pants with candy corn on them.

'I like your earrings,' I tell her, as she carefully dries the knife with a hand towel.

She holds out a dangling skeleton, blinking her eyes a couple times. 'You like em? My grandson gottem for me.'

She takes out her phone, knife in other hand.

She pulls up a picture of her grandson and shows me.

'Look at him,' she says. 'He's so fucking cute. Gah, I just . . . he's so fucking cute I just wanna . . . isn't he so cute?'

She tells me about some new action figure/show her grandson likes and how you're supposed to collect them and fight them and how she has to get the video game at her place so he could play there.

I drink the rest of my coffee, listening.

I don't have grandkids or grandparents.

What the fuck am I?

I'm simply whackin it.

'How's it going out there?' says a younger coworker, who'd started a couple days ago.

He eats a tiny bite of a dinner roll.

'We need you on 'Living Ottoman' tonight,' I say.

He laughs.

The kitchen is steamy.

Sandy returns holding an empty tray and says, 'They have ravaged my balled meat.'

*

After cocktail hour, everyone returns to the main room and takes their seats.

The bridesmaids, groomsmen, and the newlyweds come into the room again to a crowd of seated onlookers.

This is them being introduced as different people.

They've changed.

They've gone to the mountain of matrimony and returned new, whole.

They enter to loud music from the DJ.

The bride wears sunglasses and does a dance.

Groom wears matching glasses and does a similar dance.

A big moment, a moment of fame, a moment of pure attention.

Once everyone's seated, I grab a tray full of salads and walk out into the hall.

The hall is grand, open, well lit, murmuring.

The DJ plays low-volume lounge music.

He has three empty pop cans on his soundboard.

People at tables.

General mingling.

Nervous groomsman reviewing his speech on his phone.

Father of the bride collecting himself by smoothing or otherwise fastening various parts of his attire.

My coworkers and I take salads off the trays and place them before attendees.

I always have the urge to whisper, 'I touched your dressing' to guests, right into their ears, maybe kiss their earlobes a little.

But I'm a shadow.

I don't exist.

All black, apron.

Invisibled.

And that's how I like it.

We deposit salads as the father of the bride says a few words.

A few words we've all heard many times.

[Bride] is a handful.

[Groom] is just the man for her.

Or other way around.

Stories of youth.

Jokey, then a sentimental turn.

Welcome to the family.

They knew right away/They weren't sure right away.

And then when [example] happened, they knew [Groom] was serious.

She came home from [place she'd moved and interned] and there was this guy and [Wife] and I thought uh oh.

(Crowd laughs.)

But then [Groom] held the door for her getting into his [cool brand/model of car] and I knew he was an all right guy.

Then, best man/maid of honor speeches.

Couple of jokes revolving around childhood mischief, who could beat up who, the bride being boy crazy, et cetera.

'I wanted to be just like [Groom/Bride].'

Childhoods summarized.

You're my brother man, I love you.

Glad to have [Bride] for a sister.

Maid of honor crying multiple times.

'Eye'm zo happy to have [Groom] as my new brother.'

Silverware against glasses.

Best man raises his glass.

Bride and groom kiss.

People cheer.

I watch the two female bartenders watching, hands on their chests.

One of them points at me, teary-eyed, does the 'finger across the neck' thing.

A coworker wheels a coffee cart into the hall, making a subtle face to me that suggests, 'Kill them all.'

And then—it's dinnertime!

*

I carry trays of lidded dinner plates out.

I set the trays on stands and the friendlier servers unlid them and place them before guests.

Who has the beef.

Who has the veggie lasagna.

Gluten allergy.

No dairy.

Kid's meal.

I didn't have the [x], I had the [x].

This is undercooked.

We need three more salmons and a veggie lasagna.

Back and forth from the kitchen.

Coming out with full, heavy trays.

Perfect form, elegant and proud.

Hard, resolute, powerful.

A servant.

No look on my face, not a single facial muscle tensed in any way.

A scrimmage in disappearing.

'Someone bitched about the chicken,' I say, tossing lids on the meal prep counter.

Annie holds up a knife, talking to herself and making an evil face.

I help plate for a while, to catch up.

Gravy on mashed potatoes, then microgreens on top of that.

Scrappy says, 'Nice load' as she watches me ladle gravy, waiting for a tray to carry.

I breathe in loudly through my nose as I close my eyes, bite my lip, and ladle a big load of gravy onto a mound of mashed potatoes.

'Bro that's gross,' Shane says, smiling and slapping down a scoop of potatoes before sliding it over.

And after a panicked half hour, dinner is all served.

Plated, lidded, trayed, served.

Silverware against glasses.

The bride and groom kiss.

People already at the bar.

Some make the rounds at different tables.

Bride and groom take first dance.

Say hello to the new Mister and Missus.

A meaningful song.

Then [Groom] with Mom.

[Bride] with Dad.

Photographers move around for the right shot.

Sunlight catches the wood floor just the right way.

The open ceiling.

The decorations.

A look between father and bride communicates whatever.

Some people watch.

Some look at phones.

Kids hit each other.

Strays peruse the dessert table.

I'm collecting plates.

Silverware anchored, napkin covered.

Clean, with leftovers, untouched.

No one says thank you.

I touched your dressing . . . you little shit.

I carry stacks of dirty dishes, scraping significant scraps onto a top plate, then putting the empties beneath it.

Stacks.

Stacks and stacks.

Trays lifted and shouldered, carried through the narrow hallways into the kitchen.

The general dancing begins.

The bride and a three-year-old are the only ones on the floor at first.

The bride waves a doll around as the three-year-old spins in place.

An old lady in a chair nearby taps her foot, smiling.

Things are heating up.

I withdraw deeper into the shadow realm.

Stacking dirty plates on trays.

After bathroom breaks, drink retrieval, leg stretching, everyone else gradually converges on the dance floor.

Reserved at first, then the alcohol does what it does.

The music picks up.

Dance moves improvised, recalled from music videos, or simply 'just enough.'

Arms up, asses out.

Body parts all over.

A young man in a bow tie is break-dancing to a growing circle on the dance floor.

The bridesmaids, dancing together, laugh and pump their fists.

A groomsman jumps into the circle and break-dances as well.

A tie tied around his head and aviator sunglasses and drink in hand remind people that he is 'crazy.'

Cool aunts and uncles dance on the fringes, taking over when they recognize a song.

The unsuspecting, caught on the way back from the bar, do a few dance moves under duress of enthused group before shuffling off to the safety of the table, to slouch and snack.

Retreat with the old folks and out-of-shapers.

Conversing.

Coffee for some.

Nursed beers for others.

Grandma puts a Band-Aid on the foot of a small girl who has twisted and shouted on a piece of broken glass barefoot, and the girl runs back over to the side of the dance floor, where cousins take turns jump-kicking each other.

Grandma points and laughs, covering her mouth.

I explain to a coworker, as we clear the corner of the room, that partying like an old woman is ideal.

They have maybe one or two drinks, if any.

They eat sparingly, though broadly.

They dance a little.

They keep order.

They entertain, are entertained.

They leave at just the right time.

Having seen the sights, done the dos, tried the tastes, commented on the space, told a few old stories, been told a few, and left leaving *every*one wanting more.

They even probably feel *better* the next morning.

'Got that, cowboy?' says my coworker.

I wink and lift a tray full of water glasses.

I sway, hip pivoting, and sidestep the traffic, gracefully carrying the tray.

Because as long as I hold it, the tray is my baby.

I move like a feather in the wind.

Like moonlight through trees.

I move and move.

Holding many pounds of glass, I move through war zones of dancing, buzzed gesturing, kids fighting each other, and people who, simply, won't get out of the way.

I begin just walking through people.

Knocking into them with my shoulders.

I pass by Sandy in the hallway.

She spits a huge ice cube back into her plastic jar of pop, which she holds with both hands.

Smiling, she says, 'What're you doing out there, you whackin it?'

'I'm whackin it,' I say.

She tells me, gesturing with her watch, that it measured ten miles of steps last shift she worked.

'Fuck you, nerd,' I say.

She laughs.

I dump the water glasses into a plastic bin by the kitchen door, then stack the glasses into trays, carry them into the kitchen.

Shane turns around and holds out his elbow.

I bump it with mine.

'What do you see here?' he says, gesturing to a mostly empty sink area.

His face is completely serious.

Proudly serious.

'Rogue agents,' I say.

I take a break with another server, Summer, in the other reception hall, which is empty.

We polish silverware to muted dance music from the other room.

'Did three of these tubs last night,' Summer says, shaking a tub of silverware.

Butter knives, steak knives, forks, the occasional spoon, oyster fork, et cetera.

We polish and sort.

She's only a few years older than I am but already a grandmother.

She shows me pictures of her granddaughter on her phone.

Her granddaughter was born premature.

Twenty-four weeks.

She shows me with her hands how small she was when she was born.

'Like a little gerbil,' she says.

The baby was on a breathing machine.

Summer wasn't allowed to touch her.

Visited every day and watched her one-pound body hooked up to a machine.

Then one day, the baby's lung collapsed, causing the other lung to overexpand.

They gave her until the end of the day to live.

Summer said they did the handprints and everything.

Preparing for death.

But then, the baby started making a comeback.

She stabilized.

'She's such a good baby, never cries, just so happy,' Summer says, dropping a fork into a silverware holder.

I fight back tears, thinking, *Goddamnit, little baby, fight.*

Summer tells me about her daughters.

One is supposed to get married soon but her fiancé just went to jail for choking her.

I make a gun motion with thumb and forefinger and say, 'You want me to, uh . . .'

Summer talks about her last husband.

How that marriage ended.

He started drinking.

They got into an argument one night and he raised his hand.

She says she left that night with just her clothes.

Says it was hard to do but she knew she couldn't let her daughter see that happen and then do nothing.

Says her son was so scared, he walked barefoot across the street to where his grade-school principal lived, to get him for help.

Says the image of her son barefoot walking across the street in the middle of the night to get help is something she thinks about a lot.

Her reminder, she says.

A principal's job is never done, I think.

We continue polishing.

I notice Summer is staring at me, smiling.

She'd asked me out via a drunk email a couple nights before, saying she liked looking at me at work.

But was I ready to be a grandpa?

Had anyone ever gone right to grandpa?

Things to consider.

I take a piece of her gum.

She brings up sex trafficking.

She always talked about sex trafficking.

'You should walk me out to my car so I don't get sex-trafficked. It's big around here because we're right by 94. They put you in a van and shoot you up with heroin so then you CAN'T leave,' she says, grabbing my arm.

I had read about a sex trafficking situation that occurred in the dollar store parking lot by my apartment.

'All right all right,' I say.

She smiles and says, 'I'm just saying,' as she cocks her head, snaps her gum, and drops a handful of knives into a container.

We polish through an entire tub, groaning.

I laugh thinking about how important this day is for everyone out there in the hall, but not me/us; it's just work.

A shift.

A free meal and some money.

A checklist.

Not the union of two people through a vow of lifelong love.

But a series of demands.

It's the same for those attending the wedding though.

It's an itemized list from my employer, signed, a contract.

Everything you want and can pay for.

In life too, I guess.

Same for everybody.

Just another checklist.

Your checklist.

The fucking checklist.

Checklist and the eternal audition.

'All right that's IT!' I finally say, slamming down my rag.

I walk back toward the kitchen.

'Where you going?' Summer asks, laughing.

'SICK of this!' I say loudly.

My boss, putting on his coat in a closet nearby, says, 'Hey if later, you're *not* sick of it, would you maybe do trash?'

'Of course, my boy, of course!'

I go into the kitchen and cut myself a huge piece of wedding cake.

Leaning against a stainless steel counter in the kitchen, I watch the last of a magnificent sunset and eat the cake.

The sky is orange and golden, with pink in it too.

Squirrels running away.

Crows in huge numbers.

One of the event managers comes into the kitchen, putting two thumbs up and smiling.

She asks me to help her stack chairs outside from yesterday's ceremony.

Yesterday's ceremony, today's task.

'After this,' I say, holding out my cake.

She takes some of it with her fingers.

'Oh that cake sucks,' she says, grimacing.

But she's hated every cake I can remember.

There are people who will always hate the cake.

Don't listen to them.

Don't listen to the people who always like the cake either.

We go outside and stack all the chairs as it gets dark.

Blue, then darker blue.

Dark and damp.

Slipping on the wet grass.

Michigan.

Beautiful Midwest Mother.

'Don't forget they're doing that sparkler send-off thing,' the manager says.

It's where we light sparklers for the family and they stand on either side of a walkway for the newlyweds to walk through, with a limo waiting at the end to take them away.

'Yay,' I say.

We stack and carry chairs for another half hour.

Whackin it.

*

Back inside, the effort carries on, though increasingly subdued.

Alcohol.

Powered by, then fading from.

Exhaustion.

Arguments.

Conversations.

Plans for tomorrow/rest of weekend.

Nothing left to do.

Dancing.

Desserts.

Coffee.

Water.

Phones babysit bored kids.

The sugar is gone.

Thrill of dress up has become the irritability of being in uncomfortable clothes.

The flower girl sleeps in her mom's arms, jacketed.

Conversational pairs around the bar, corners of the room.

The audition nears its inevitable end.

The DJ does his best.

A committed number continue dancing.

Broken glasses.

A groomsman sleeps facedown in the corner of the room on one hand.

A drunk bridesmaid sits in a chair with her bare feet up on another chair as someone rubs her neck.

A woman in a beautiful dress cries near the bathroom, consoled by another.

The bathrooms are a mess.

I take a clean length of paper towel in the bathroom and pick up wet paper towels off the ground.

I sweep up broken glass.

I bus with the other servers for a while, carrying out a few last trays of cake slices.

But the dessert table is abandoned slowly, like all else.

Check-marked.

Tried, photographed.

Eventually, the DJ announces the last shuttle, calls last call for the bar, and plays the last song.

We herd most of the people outside for the send-off.

The event coordinator and I pass out sparklers in the darkness.

We assist with long lighters.

A bridesmaid has trouble holding her sparkler in my flame.

'Keep it together now,' I say smiling.

'Stopppp I'm tryingggggg,' she says.

Then it finally erupts.

Others follow.

White/gold flames sparkle out in the night.

'I'm gonna shove five of these up my nephew's ass,' says the father of the bride.

'Thang you for this, Don,' says another bridesmaid, red-eyed and tired, a man's coat over her shoulders.

'You were lovely, Krissy,' says the father of the bride, eyeing his sparklers' spray, taking his place in the procession.

The limo's brake lights glow in the distance.

Moon high and full and bright.

I look up to a lit window of the reception hall, watching a co-worker's head move around.

It's all very good.

My heart is full.

'There they are, woooo!' yells someone as the bride and groom exit the building.

Everyone starts to yell, holding up their sparklers.

Loud cheering.

Waving.

Sparkling.

Kisses.

The couple walks down the sparkling path, smiling, hand in hand.

Faces kissed, shoulders patted, smiles returned.

Down the path into the limo, waving goodbye.

Everyone will talk soon.

Thank you for coming.

Attendees dump their sparklers into buckets of water, or onto the grass.

Family hugs.

'I love you man,' a man says after a hug. 'One more.'

They hug again.

Dad walks Grandma arm in arm back toward the building.

She says it was a lovely party.

She's glad she wore sensible shoes.

Someone will take her to the hotel.

When I get back inside, a few stragglers still claim the reception hall.

Decorations and bottles in hand.

Tieless.

Women shoeless.

Confused about the remainder of the mission.

'Did we miss the uh sparkler thing?'

Who's going where.

How do you get there.

Did you find my phone.

I think Colin has it.

A bridesmaid sways, holding her purse in both arms.

Her eyes are unfocused, accusing.

'What are we doing?' she says.

Sandy whispers, 'You're getting the fuck out of here, bitch.'

We laugh, too loud.

We follow the group out of the room, glassware in our arms.

When I pass the staircase, I hear this terrible slapping/pounding sound.

And I look down the stairs.

It's a bridesmaid backward-somersaulting down the stairs.

She tumbles down the stairs with terrible thumps, landing at the bottom.

As her head hits the concrete floor, it makes the sound of shattering glass.

Green-tinted pieces where her head once was.

Red wine spreads across the ground.

People rush to help as the red wine spreads through the pieces.

'I'm a nurse, back up back up,' says someone, handing off a sleeping child.

It's okay she's okay just everybody back up.

A couple people help the bridesmaid up and carry her out to the shuttle and everything goes back to normal.

Shane sweeps up the broken glass into a dustpan.

Sandy asks me if she died.

'Your mom died when I came inside her.'

She laughs hard.

She wipes her eye and says she just wants to get the fuck out of there.

Yeah.

Summer says she just wants to take off her shoes.

Says that's all she thinks about.

Not food, booze, drugs, sex, none of that, just taking her shoes off.

Yeah.

We stack chairs, wipe tables, carry and rearrange tables, sweep, mop, collect decorations.

Everyone puts leftover flowers in their hair or buttonholes of their shirts.

We throw out name cards.

Plastic cups.

Goodbye, flowers.

Goodbye, garland.

Goodbye, candles.

Armload after armload.

Into the black plastic bags.

Yesterday's ceremony is today's task.

The flowers are in the trash.

The cake is gone.

All the songs over.

Sweeping the entire hall.

Electronic candles, plastic forks, some Polaroids, a few streamers, broken glass, flower parts, all swept.

Scraping wax off tables with our drivers' licenses.

Spraying and wiping the tables.

Ears ringing from the music.

Eating leftover desserts off the dessert table.

A sinfully delectable moment.

A rotten luxury.

'I swear I told myself if I didn't get some of that dessert somebody had to die,' says a coworker, staring.

Others agree.

We stand around for a second, eating dessert.

Vultures.

'Everybody have fun tonight?' I say.

We finish moving tables.

Stacking and unstacking chairs.

Setting up rows for tomorrow's ceremony.

Tomorrow's ceremony is tonight's work.

My coworkers begin leaving one by one.

Bye.

Don't get sex-trafficked.

I stay behind to finish mopping the staircase.

Dragging the mop side to side.

The reception hall has become cold.

Not enough bodies.

Sky outside, black, with the faint fog of some streetlight.

Town quiet.

Everyone asleep.

Shit is perfect.

AAAAAooOOOOOoooOoo.

'Quit whackin it,' Sandy says, coming down the staircase.

She holds out a small dessert thing she says she was saving for her girlfriend but.

'Your mom's my girlfriend,' I say.

See you tomorrow.

Yeah, see you tomorrow.

*

When I get off, I go out the back exit and through the parking lot.

It's dark and quiet.

I can see my breath.

There's no one else out.

Just cold, wet, leaf-plastered sidewalk.

I put my hood on.

The moments between getting off work and getting home.

There's none more powerful than I at that moment.

You can take anything that's mine except this.

A trophy—albeit invisible—that I hold up high, on top of an infinite mountain, smiling.

End of the audition.

Freedom.

Defined by its opposite on either end.

All homes quiet for me, stars sparkling for me, the air blowing around just to touch me.

My heart welling up, eyes glowing, hair standing on end.

I turn into bats and fly away.

I become a deer and flee.

Exiting my own body as my breath and disappearing.

Reappearing as a star.

Whackin it.

I walk down the main drag of town, with its one bar, a couple antique places, and a butcher.

A couple people from the wedding smoke cigarettes in front of the bar.

Oh lord.

I pass the sole gas station, with the whoevers from wherever going wherever buying whatever for whatever.

The four-way intersection, red lights blinking at this point in the night.

Down the blocks.

What's going on, everyone.

Halloween decorations in windows, bikes on lawns, trucks, a dead raccoon in the gutter, the night sky, black with stars.

Smell of burning leaves.

Another winter on its way.

Comforting, deep within me.

Yes.

Part of a process.

Bigger than me.

More power in the grain of one second of one of the millions and billions of days yet to happen than in a million of my lifetimes.

There is more.

There is always more than this.

I imagine Summer's premature grandchild at the center of the earth, hooked up to a machine, making a tiny fist.

No longer dying, only just now beginning to live.

A mind, tiny lungs, a beating heart.

I shiver.

Sniff.

Think about how the coat I'm wearing was my grandpa's.

My grandma gave it to me after he died.

I want someone to have it after I die.

I imagine snapping my fingers and the coat shrinks to very small and I put it on Summer's premature baby and it immediately becomes very strong, flexing her way off of various machines and IVs.

My block is very quiet.

The wind blows some leaves down the street.

When I get to my apartment complex, I look at it, and it looks back.

Some units lit by TV but mostly dim or completely dark.

Yes, hello friend.

I go to put my key in the front door.

But no.

Not yet.

I can't.

For some reason, I just can't.

So instead, I walk around to the back of the building.

Through the field of dying lavender, lit by cobwebby moonlight.

Wind blowing.

End-of-the-world shit.

I walk toward the woods with crunching steps.

Bugs chirping and murmuring.

A red light blinking atop a powerline many miles away says yes, keep going.

It says I'll see you there.

It says, I'm already with you.

When I get to the woods, it's so dark I can barely see, except for one of the entrances, which is even darker.

So I walk in, stumbling a few times over roots and fallen branches.

I'm dizzy.

All kinds of things scurrying and making noise in the darkness.

But then, the moonlight adjusts, outlining branches and fallen limbs.

And I walk without direction.

Enjoying the clean, cold air.

Until I get to a clearing.

It's a clearing I didn't know about.

The moon above—huge, low, and bone white.

And there, in the middle of the clearing, a great stag.

Tall and proud, beautiful and strong.

With huge, sharp antlers.

Big black eyes, dewed with moon-glow.

Breathing steam.

It sees me right away, but doesn't move, just stands there breathing.

So beautiful.

You're so beautiful.

Just stares back, turning its head sideways to get a good look.

Yes.

I sniff.

It lowers its head, steam blowing out of its nostrils.

Snorting.

The stag begins to kick the ground a little with its front hoof.

Huffing.

But I just stand there.

Steam our only exchange.

Tension.

My ears ring in the cold dark.

Eyes watering, nose numb.

I feel enormous.

Totally enormous and free.

More than alive.

Each blood cell, a lit sparkler.

There is more than this.

And I matter absolutely, until I don't.

One lung collapses and the other expands to help.

The wheels come off the track on a sharp turn, but we're gonna get it right.

We're gonna be all right.

'Boo!' I say.

And the stag kicks the ground one more time before running.

It runs right at me.

Sprinting, head down.

But I stand my ground.

And the horns go into my chest.

I exhale sharply, immediately weakened, grabbing the horns.

Warm blood pours out onto my hands.

Onto the horns and head of the stag, steaming in the moonlight.

Through my throat and out of my mouth, into my beard and down my neck.

I try to make a sound but it's just like eccckkkk.

And everything gets colder as the edges go.

I slump to the ground—wet dirt on my face the last thing I feel as the stag walks back into the darkness.

EPILOGUE

Robby

I hadn't talked to Robby in a while.

We'd lapsed again.

But I was going back to Chicago for a couple days.

First time I'd been back in years.

And it was right around his birthday, so I figured I'd text him.

I messaged him 'Happy Birthday, saucemaster,' and asked him what he was doing.

He said he'd skipped work and was going fishing at Humboldt Park if I wanted to come by.

So when my train got in, I rented a bike and rode over to Humboldt.

The streets were still mostly empty.

Morning reaching pace.

Cafe workers putting out chairs for restaurants along the Division Street strip.

Last night's rain in small puddles, to steam through the day.

Middle of summer.

Puerto Rican flags hung everywhere for the coming parade weekend.

I hadn't thought much about Chicago.

But there it was.

And it all came back to me.

Not all of it good.

Not all of it bad.

But all of it.

When I got to the park, I took a path toward the lagoon.

There were city workers discussing things in neon yellow shirts.

Measuring.

Pointing.

Few kids on the playground, nannies standing watch.

Sticks on the ground from the storms the night before.

People setting up carts to sell shirts and flags and food.

Airbrushed T-shirts.

Some homeless people, dancing off the last of the previous night's drunk, or retuning.

Playing dominoes.

I passed by a marshy area.

There was a blackbird perched on a stake.

The blackbird was beautiful.

It turned its head to look at me as I neared.

Then flew off the stake, coming right at me, screaming.

I couldn't see it for a second, but felt a scratch on top of my head as my hair ruffled.

And for a moment, I'll admit it, I felt true terror.

I was terrified.

Whatever the blackbird was trying to do, it worked.

I laughed.

Hell, I got it.

Nice work, friend.

You win today, friend.

I found Robby in a nook off the main area of the lagoon, with two poles in the water, drinking a beer.

'Ah, the North American Asshole,' I said.

He laughed and turned around.

I said happy birthday and we hugged.

'Good to see you,' I said.

'Good to see you,' he said, smiling.

We stood by the water and looked out.

The lagoon was covered in lily pads and white flowers.

A breeze blew through the trees.

A cloud cover, but still very bright.

Seemed like a day that wouldn't ever really get going.

And that was fine.

I left my pole in the water unattended.

Robby reeled in his line, struggling with a lily pad a little, then whipping the line back into a tree, where he had to untangle it.

Told me he was fishing for catfish, which he'd caught there before.

I told him about the blackbird.

'Fucked me up,' I said.

Robby laughed, slapping his thigh.

Talked about how in the blackbird's mind that must've been the right thing to do.

And to some degree it was.

Because for that split second, I was very intimidated.

I . . . got the message.

'They're probably mating,' I said.

'Or guarding eggs,' said Robby.

Then he talked about how that's intimidating, yeah, but like, he explained, you know, if I/we were blackbird egg hunters, or whatever, we'd have no problem.

Like ultimately, we had the power.

Yeah.

'Sometimes you just gotta remember that,' I said vaguely.

We looked out at the water for a while, catching nothing.

After a while, Robby switched from bait to a lure.

He explained the lure he was using.

It was a neon-colored octopus thing.

He showed me a small amount of what looked like broom bristle material, covering the hook.

It kept the hook from catching on lily pads, but was easily disengaged if something bit, exposing the hook.

'I mean, it looks like something I'd eat,' he said. 'Let's see if it works.'

Different kinds of lures.

Different ways to catch fish.

Although, Robby explained, it didn't really matter, because fish will eat anything.

A fish will eat anything smaller than it, he said.

They're sick bastards.

Fish will eat their own offspring, frogs, anything smaller.

'People say it's a dog-eat-dog world,' Robby said. 'But it's more of a fish-eat-fish world.'

We stood there in silence for a while.

Robby smoked a cigarette.

Some kids yelled at the playground nearby.

The park got busy.

People playing soccer, bicyclists, paletas salesmen, dominoes/ chess games.

Humboldt Park.

Robby said his wife usually accompanied him fishing, reading recipe magazines and asking him why he keeps reeling in lily pads.

'She doesn't know shit,' he said, laughing. 'She always asks why it's not a fish.'

I stared at the line right where it went into the water.

Robby explained how the fish should be happy he's the one who catches them.

Because he always puts them back, and he knows how to take out a hook.

A blue crane swooped down and landed near the lagoon.

'Ey look at this guy,' I said.

We watched the crane poke around bushes for food.

It began to rain a little and we moved back beneath some trees, both poles left unmanned in the water.

I watched a spider climbing back up into a tree.

Fuck this shit, it's raining!

I imagined the spider crouched beneath a leaf, just waiting.

The sun came out just a little.

A rainbow connected the sky to the lagoon.

Robby reeled in then cast again.

I worried about him pulling the line back and hooking my eye.

Seemed not only possible, but likely.

When the rain let up, we stepped back out.

The clouds moved on and it was very bright.

A mother duck and her babies swam into our area of the lagoon.

The babies were small and soft feathered, glowing in the sunlight.

'Fish'll eat baby ducks too, man,' said Robby. 'Especially the bigger fish. They're bastards. People say dog-eat-dog, but it's more fish-eat-fish.'

I watched the ducks swimming around the lily pads.

Gently dividing the murky water.

It went from feeling like a day that'd never get going, to one that'd never end.

And that was fine too.